Dear Hannah

Books by Thomas Hauser

Nonfiction:
  Missing
  The Trial of Patrolman Thomas Shea
  For Our Children (with Frank Macchiarola)
  The Family Legal Companion
  The Black Lights

Fiction:
  Ashworth & Palmer
  Agatha's Friends
  The Beethoven Conspiracy
  Hanneman's War
  The Fantasy
  Dear Hannah

THOMAS HAUSER

Dear Hannah

TOR

DEAR HANNAH

Copyright © 1987 by Thomas Hauser

All rights reserved, including the right to reproduce this book or portions thereof in any form.

Grateful acknowledgment is made for permission to reprint from the following material:

"Unchained Melody" by Hy Zaret and Alex North; © 1955 by Frank Music Corp.; © renewed 1983 by Frank Music Corp.; international copyright secured; all rights reserved; used by permission.

"Stardust" by Mitchell Parish and Hoagy Carmichael; © 1929 by Mills Music, Inc. Copyright renewed; used with permission; all rights reserved.

First printing: March 1987

A TOR Book

Published by Tom Doherty Associates, Inc.
49 West 24 Street
New York, N.Y. 10010

ISBN: 0-312-93005-4

Library of Congress Catalog Card Number: 86-50960

Printed in the United States of America

0 9 8 7 6 5 4 3 2 1

For Lise and Bob

PART ONE

PART ONE

Chapter 1

ETHEL HATED BLOOMINGDALE'S. IT WAS TOO BIG and too crowded, and she always felt as though she had to dress well and put on makeup just to walk through the door. The carnival atmosphere, the noise—she was intimidated by it all. Every salesperson seemed determined to spray her with perfume, swab on sample lotions, or turn her eyelids blue. And the place was overrun by fashionably dressed, beautiful women infinitely more desirable than she was.

"Be sophisticated," she told herself as she passed through the Lexington Avenue entrance into the store. "You're twenty-nine years old, intelligent, and a graduate of Bryn Mawr. Don't be so insecure."

Still, as she made her way past several display cases filled with ladies' watches, up a short flight of stairs to the main floor, she felt remarkably unpoised. The place was madness. Escalators to the left, perfume to the right; beyond the perfume, seemingly endless

9

rows of counters stocked with makeup and toilet articles. Don't make eye contact with the other shoppers! Don't stare! Half the Eileen Ford modeling agency seemed to be there. Great legs, cover girl features—all in contrast with Ethel's somewhat pretty face and heavy thighs.

"Men's ties?" she asked a salesgirl.

"Straight ahead, at the rear of the store."

Still intimidated, Ethel moved past counter after counter laden with lipsticks, powders, colognes, rouges, gels, moisturizers, lotions, cleaning agents, and bath oils. Part of her leaned toward dropping a trail of bread crumbs so she could get out when she was done.

Keep going. Pajamas. Men's shirts; Yves Saint Laurent, Calvin Klein, Vincente Nesi, Pierre Cardin. Further on, at the very back of the store, she found men's ties, an island of relative calm by the Third Avenue door. There were endless rows of ties on spindles and in showcases under glass. Ties with dots, ties with squiggles. Father had gone to Harvard. Mother had instructed Ethel to pick out a tie for his fortieth reunion. "School colors; not too flashy."

After appropriate deliberation, Ethel centered her attention on a crimson tie with evenly spaced thin white stripes. Picking it off the counter, she held it to the light and, for the first time, noticed the young man standing next to her.

"That's a nice tie," he said.

"Thank you."

He didn't follow up. She didn't pursue it. He drifted away. Kind of cute, Ethel decided. Five-ten, maybe a bit taller, pleasant face, mid-thirties, brown hair. She was a little annoyed with herself for letting him go. Had he been interested in her? Of course he was interested, dummy. Men don't just go around admiring ties.

She paid for the tie. Twenty dollars plus sales tax, which came to a total of $21.65. That was another problem with Blooming-dale's; it was expensive. Then she went back to the middle of the store, waited in line for the tie to be gift-wrapped, and finally escaped out onto Third Avenue leaving Bloom-ingdale's behind, thinking it hadn't been so bad.

Except when she reached the curb, the guy who admired ties was there.

"Are you following me?"

"Sort of," he answered.

What to say next? "You're a liar" wasn't appropriate, since he was telling the truth. And if Ethel was going to be truthful herself, her social life hadn't been all that great lately and the guy was cute.

"Define 'sort of,' " she demanded.

"Actually, I was in the store. I saw you

and—what can I say; I liked the way you look. . . . My name is Arnold Tinsley."

"Hello, Arnold. My name is Ethel Purcell."

Not two of the great names of all time, Ethel told herself. There was Arnold Stang, Arnold Schwarzenegger; Ethel Kennedy, Ethel Merman, Ethel Barrymore.

"Would you like to take a walk?"

"I guess so," she answered.

After all, she had to meet people some way in New York, and Bloomingdale's was as good a place as any. She wondered if Arnold had been looking for someone more fashionable than she was, struck out, and then settled for her.

"Where would you like to go?"

"Up Third Avenue," she told him.

That way, if the conversation turned dull, when they hit the Seventies, she'd be home. Except—surprise—it wasn't dull. She liked him! As they walked, it became apparent that Arnold Tinsley was nice, kind of cute, and bright. Once, he even made her laugh.

"Most people send postcards when they travel on vacation," he told her. "My mother goes to Europe, and two days after she leaves I get an envelope stuffed full of vending machine life insurance policies."

"I know what you mean. Whenever I travel, I call my parents as soon as I get home. My mother is always worried about a plane crash. I could take a bus, and she'd worry about a plane crashing on top of the bus."

Kindred spirits; a nice guy. They walked up Third Avenue until they reached 71st Street, a half block from Ethel's apartment.

"Would you like to come up for a cup of coffee?"

"Sure."

Ethel lived on the fourth floor. There was no doorman. They took the elevator. Inside the apartment, she offered him something to drink and he chose orange juice.

"Sit wherever you're comfortable," she told him.

He took a chair, not the sofa—another indication that he wasn't a masher.

"My mother is really something," Arnold said, returning to already-tested terrain. "Last month, she called and asked if I'd been in a coma because I hadn't called for a week."

"I know the feeling. My—"

Then Ethel saw the knife.

"If you come any closer, I'll scream."

It was foolish to say, because it took at least two seconds to get the words out of her mouth and by then the palm of his hand was across her face, and what she should have done was just screamed. Not that it would have made any difference.

It was happening. Things like this really happened. Ethel felt the knife. It was happening to her.

□ □ □

No one had wanted Hannah. And then suddenly it seemed as though everyone was pushing and crowding just to get close to her. But it wasn't her fault; none of it. Being unwanted had started before she could remember much of anything at all.

When Hannah was two, her father died. Perfect timing to screw up a child, although Hannah figured that, where the death of a parent was concerned, any age could do the job. For the next year, whenever her mother had left home, the same dialogue would occur between parent and child.

"Mommy come home—please!"

"Mommy will come home. I promise." ᛉ

Six days before Hannah's third birthday, a drunk driver ran a stoplight and Mommy didn't come home. The police notified the baby-sitter, put Hannah in a squad car, and drove her forty miles to her grandparents' house. Even now, at age thirty-five, Hannah remembered the look on her grandmother's face when she was told by the police that her daughter had died. There was grief and pain, followed by the realization that someone had to take care of Hannah, and that she and Grandpa were the ones.

Hannah stood there, six days shy of her third birthday, clutching her teddy bear, frightened and confused. Grandma looked directly at her for what seemed an eternity, then muttered, "Oh, shit. I don't want this child."

The mansion that Hannah grew up in with her grandparents was in northern Ohio. Grandpa was a banker who'd inherited too much money and, during the course of his life, added a great deal more. Grandma came from a socially prominent family and understood the material things in life quite well. The mansion had been built in the early 1900s facing Lake Hume, and had three floors divided into eight bedrooms, a living room the size of most restaurants, a dining room, kitchen, pantry, and servants' quarters. The grounds were landscaped and in full bloom from April through September. An L-shaped porch fronted two sides of the mansion and, because the house was on a hill, the porch afforded a perfect view of the surrounding environs. Summer nights before dinner, Grandma and Grandpa would sit outside, drinks in hand, watching the sun set over the shimmering lake through the green leaves of the trees.

Hannah wasn't allowed. During sunset hours, the porch was for adults only. Nor was Hannah allowed to have friends in the house or use her grandparents' last name. "You're Hannah Wade," they told her. "That was the name given to you when you were born. We're your grandparents, not your mother

15

and father. Our name is Milburn. Your mother and father up in heaven would be very upset if you changed your name."

When Hannah was four, she caught a fish in the lake, proclaimed it her pet, and kept it in a large washtub behind the garage. Grandma instructed the maid to cook it for dinner and, when the maid demurred, cooked it herself. One November morning, with a thin coating of snow on the ground, Hannah awoke to her grandfather's touch. "Look out the window at what Grandpa brought you." Outside, strung from a tree, was a freshly killed deer, bleeding from a bullet in the brain.

They punished Hannah for being alive. They split her open and tore at her insides. They didn't care if she lived or died. And then, at age six, when Hannah didn't think she could stand any more, she discovered Miss Bridges and her whole world turned around. Because Miss Bridges loved her. And Miss Bridges taught Hannah to dance.

They met at school the week before Hannah's Christmas vacation began. Rebecca Bridges had come to an assembly with a film of *The Nutcracker* to explain ballet and recruit students for dance lessons at her studio nearby. Relatively little was known about her. She was from New York, had studied ballet with someone named Balanchine, was forty years old, never married, and had moved recently to Ohio. She lived with another woman whom people mistakenly assumed was a platonic friend.

The Nutcracker was pure magic, the most beautiful thing Hannah had ever seen. She looked at the dancers, and wanted to be like them. Soon after, the lessons with Miss Bridges began. At first, they were limited to simple exercises and moving to music with correct technique. For a child her age, Hannah's attention span was extraordinary. Ages seven and eight saw a more disciplined version of her earlier training and working muscles into basic positions. At nine and ten, the combinations grew more complex, more physically and mentally demanding. At eleven, Hannah went on toe.

Very few children have talent as dancers. Hannah was a star. Ballet to her was a world of swans and flowers, a wonderful escape from the ugliness that had scarred her life. Rebecca Bridges became her "mother"; fellow dancers were her only friends. She buried herself in the tortuous routine of impossible positions and contorted limbs, training her muscles in ballet's unnatural ways. She lived in two worlds. At home, she experienced migraine headaches; instead of a bed, she slept on the floor. Dancing, she was a prima ballerina, long hair worn up as her lithe figure swirled across the floor.

In school, Hannah was an enigma to her peers. They knew her only as someone who came to class, got better grades than they did, and lived in a mansion overlooking Lake Hume. No one could penetrate the haunting visage that concealed her inner self. Around the age that boys started to get interested in girls, it was agreed that Hannah was beautiful, but she was strangely unapproachable and everyone kept their distance. By tenth grade, she was the heartthrob of the entire male population at Davis High School. Five feet five inches tall; 110 pounds; long brown hair; flawless features. Hannah Wade was the most beautiful girl any of the students had ever seen, and a sizable portion of the male faculty lusted after her as well. The consensus of her classmates was that she had every physical attribute possible except large breasts. Then she got breasts—B cup, perfectly shaped and round. And she hated them; because ballet is a visual art, looks count. Talent isn't enough; a dancer's proportions have to be just right, and Hannah's breasts threatened her career. There were no classical dancers with big tits. Her entire life was in jeopardy if her breasts continued to grow.

Thank God, they stopped. A little large, but manageable. Hannah finished high school, and when she graduated, Rebecca Bridges (who was dying of cancer) arranged for her to come to New York and audition for the American Ballet Theatre. She passed, of course. Star quality was written all over her. No one had ever looked more glamorous in a sweaty leotard; even her stone calluses and blackened toenails looked good. But infinitely more important was the fact that, as a dancer, Hannah was as close to perfect as a seventeen-year-old with her limited background could be.

Four years of rigorous training followed. Rebecca Bridges died, as did Hannah's grandmother. One death was mourned; the other wasn't. For a while, Hannah lived with a graduate student who was madly in love with her, but after eight months she moved out. All of her energy was devoted to dance. She didn't have time for lovers. Then came age twenty-one, when Hannah's career was at a breakthrough point—the moment an artist lives for.

And then came the back spasms.

Most people have five lumbar vertebrae at the base of their spine and, beneath them, seven more vertebrae fused together to form their sacrum and coccyx. After the doctors finished their tests, they told Hannah that in her case there was a slight misalignment. "It's a fairly common condition," they explained. "Most people who suffer from it aren't even aware that the condition exists."

Most people aren't dancers. First, Hannah tried physical therapy; then she tried forcing herself to dance with pain. But the spasms grew worse, and at age twenty-two she was

19

forced to acknowledge that her career was over before it had really begun. Given the severity of her physical problem, no one could understand what had driven her as far as she had come.

The next thirteen years didn't really matter. That was what Hannah told herself sometimes when she felt particularly down. She'd gotten married to a man whose way of shaking hands with a woman was to run his eyes across her chest. The only time he treated her like a lover was when they were in bed together, and after ten months they were divorced. Other men followed, but whatever the relationship, Hannah was always looking for something else.

Her grandfather died and left her no money. To support herself—and because she loved it—she began to teach ballet to children. Without a college diploma, there wasn't much else she thought she could do. Often, she wished she could bring Rebecca Bridges back—even if it were just for a day—to talk, to ask her about life. Because life was too complicated. One of the things Hannah had learned from ballet was that nothing is ever completely right. There's always a pirouette that's too slow, or an angle that's one degree off. Probably life was the same way, but to be thirty-five, lonely, a virtual orphan and unloved was too much to tolerate. Maybe there wasn't any answer. Maybe instead of dealing with cosmic questions like life and death and happiness and love, she should start with small things—answer the immediate questions—like, what the hell is this?

Safely ensconced in her apartment, Hannah stared at the cardboard box on the kitchen table in front of her. Most likely, it was a prank. She was being silly; there was no reason to be frightened, but the package scared her. It had come in the mail, wrapped in plain brown paper with her name and address printed on the front. There was no return address. Inside was the withered brownish-green shaft of a long-stemmed rose with the head cut off. And pierced by a thorn was a plain white card with crude letters that read *THHIRWRDNK*.

□   □   □

All day long, Richard Marritt had felt trouble coming. Nineteen years as a cop, the last eleven as a detective on Manhattan's Upper West Side, had given him a sixth sense for that sort of thing. The day itself had been largely routine. At seven A.M. he'd kissed his wife good-bye and taken the subway into Manhattan from his home in Queens. For most of the ride, he'd fantasized about being a major league baseball player. Once or twice, he thought two months ahead to June, when his twenty years on the force would expire and he'd be eligible to retire on three-quarters pension. Still, being a cop was something Marritt did well. It was his job. When all was said and done, he knew he wouldn't retire.

At the precinct house, the detective spent several hours shuffling papers in a second-floor office before conferring with Jim Dema, the fourth-year patrolman assigned to him on a regular basis. They were vastly different from one another but worked well as a team. Marritt was forty-four years old, five-foot-ten, heavyset with thick black hair, the proud father of two sons, Jonathan and David, ages ten and eight respectively. Dema was twenty years younger, tall and slim with sand-colored hair—and gay. Learning about his partner's sexual preference had bothered Marritt, and at first he hadn't wanted to work with Dema. But the younger cop kept doing his job well, and finally Marritt had come to terms with the notion.

After lunch, Marritt went back to his paper work. Shortly before two o'clock, another detective came by, seeking advice on an upcoming drug bust. At two-thirty, Marritt's wife called and asked him to stop at Zabar's on the way home. "I know we have delicatessens in Queens," she told him. "But the Scotch salmon at Zabar's is supposed to be special. Bring home some prosciutto too," she added.

"What's wrong with the Kew Gardens Deli?"

"Please; just do it, Richard."

Don't argue, the detective told himself. The marriage had been working pretty well lately; not exciting, but comfortable. Some couples create triangles to avoid dealing directly with each other. Whatever happened, he and his wife could always talk.

Marritt got off duty at five o'clock. Walking west from the precinct house, he bought a copy of the *New York Post* before proceeding to 80th Street, where Zabar's occupied three storefronts on the west side of Broadway. Inside the delicatessen, the smell of freshly ground coffee filled the air. Pots, pans, and sausages hung from above. The place was jammed, too many people pressing forward to occupy too few spaces. Making his way past a maze of cheeses, the detective came to the deli counter at the rear of the store. Numbers were being called over a loud-speaker: "Sixty-four . . . sixty-five . . ." Marritt looked around, saw a number dispenser at the end of the counter, went over, and pulled out number seventy-nine. That meant there were fourteen people ahead of him. Annoyed, and with nothing better to do, he opened his newspaper and began to read. A Brooklyn man had won two million dollars in the state lottery. The Pentagon had paid $659 for a plastic ashtray and $435 for a hammer. A twenty-nine-year-old woman had been stabbed to death in her apartment on Manhattan's East Side. Focusing on the last story, Marritt looked at the accompanying photograph of the victim, then the text:

> A 29-year-old brokerage house employee was found brutally stabbed to death last night in her one-bedroom apartment at 310 East 71st Street in Manhattan. Police said that the body of Ethel Purcell was discovered after a friend telephoned the building superintendent to report—

"Seventy-three . . . seventy-four . . ." The delicatessen number count continued.

Marritt finished the article, reflecting on the fact that mankind as a whole might be a nice concept but sometimes the individual parts weren't so hot. He was glad the murder had happened in another precinct. Finally, his number came up, and a white-aproned counter attendant who looked like Ed Koch gestured for him to order.

"Half a pound of prosciutto, please."

"What kind?"

"Regular, I guess."

"There's no such thing. We got San Pietro prosciutto, Wolf prosciutto, Citterio prosciutto . . ." The litany continued, ending with, "Mister, I'll make it easy for you. Do you want domestic or imported?"

"Imported, I think," Marritt answered.

"You got it."

While the prosciutto was being sliced, Marritt surveyed the fare on display behind the counter. Stuffed eggplant, pasta primavera, ratatouille, gnocci in pesto sauce, twenty different kinds of pâté. The choices were endless.

"And half a pound of Scotch salmon," he instructed when the prosciutto was wrapped.

"Sorry, that's a different counter."

Glancing at his watch, grumbling, the detective crossed the floor, took another number, and repeated the waiting process, this time at the fish counter. Finally, a half hour after he'd entered Zabar's, he made his way to a row of cash registers by the front door. Three registers were open. He opted for the one in the middle because the last two couples on that line seemed together, which meant the line would move faster. Both men in the foursome were in their mid-fifties, the women a few years younger. Marritt assumed the couples were married. One of the women left the line while her counterpart and the two men continued talking. They were loud and, judging by the jewelry they wore, rich. One of the men, referred to as "Bernie" by his companions, was wearing a checked sports jacket and diamond pinkie ring. He was the loudest. When Bernie reached the cash register, he asked the checkout girl for a loaf of rye bread, sliced, which took another two

25

minutes. Then, after the bill was totaled, his wife reappeared with several more items.

"And one croissant," Bernie added.

The checkout clerk totaled the new items, added the croissant, and announced that the bill was forty-eight dollars and seven cents. Bernie reached for his wallet.

"What do you think you're doing?" the other man in the foursome demanded.

"Paying."

"Not tonight. This is my treat."

By now, Marritt had been in Zabar's for three quarters of an hour. The debate over who should pay lasted another few minutes. Finally, Bernie relented. "All right, Henry. But next time it's on me."

Henry paid with his American Express card, which meant the register clerk had to write the order up, which consumed another three minutes. Then, when everything was squared away, an announcement came over the loudspeaker: "Ladies and gentlemen—attention all shoppers. As a special value, Zabar's is now offering croissants, regularly priced at eighty-nine cents, for only sixty-nine cents. Pick some up at the checkout counter before you leave the store."

Bernie stood there, eyeing the checkout clerk.

"Oh, shit," Marritt muttered. "Here it comes."

"Listen, sweetheart. We just paid close to

fifty dollars. Aren't we entitled to a discount on the croissant?"

The clerk shrugged. "I'm sorry, sir. The discount applies only to croissants bought after the announcement."

"Maybe that's true for some people, but I'm sure the discount is applicable to customers like us."

Marritt looked at his watch. Fifty-five minutes and counting.

"I'm sorry, sir. Store policy is very clear on that point."

"In that case, I'd like to speak to the store manager. Maybe we can change the policy."

"Sir, I assure you—"

"Sweetheart, I don't want your assurance. I want our twenty cents back. And—"

Marritt couldn't take any more. "Mister," he interrupted, "you bought your food; you paid for it. Now, why don't you just get out of the way and let the lady do her job."

"What's it to you?"

"I want to go home is what it is to me. And for what it's worth to you, I'm a cop, so don't start mouthing off." Wearily, the detective reached into his pocket and took out a quarter. "Look, Bernie, here's twenty-five cents. Do me a favor. Take it, forget about your discount, and keep the change."

"And he kept it," Marritt told his wife that night. "The son of a bitch kept the change."

TWO MONTHS LATER. A TUESDAY IN JUNE. LATE-
afternoon sunlight filtered through the dance
studio. Dressed in a black leotard and tights,
Hannah Wade stood in the center of the room
with ten girls ages six through eight clus-
tered around her. Like their mentor, the
children wore leotards, tights, and Capezio
shoes, soft leather with bands of elastic across
the arches. In time, some would graduate to
toe shoes, but going on toe too early could
ruin a child's feet; thus the slippers.

The room was spacious and well lit, twenty-
four feet square, on the second floor of a loft
building in lower Manhattan. One wall was
fully mirrored adjacent to a long oak barre. A
second, smaller room was reserved for parents-
in-waiting, who weren't allowed in the studio
while a lesson was underway. Hannah rented
the studio for two hours a day, five days a
week, at twenty dollars an hour. Averaging
ten students a lesson at eight dollars each,
she cleared $30,000 a year. Not bad for what

was essentially a part-time job, but she earned every penny. The children loved her, and she was good.

"All right, girls, warm-up exercises. Diana, get rid of your gum. No fooling around. Four pliés in first position. . . . Stephanie, keep your head up. . . . Daniele, stand up straight; bring your backside in."

After fifteen minutes of exercises, Hannah moved to the center of the room to demonstrate combinations. Then, one at a time, she corrected the children as they sought to emulate what she had done. "Gita, that's very good, but follow your leading arm with your head a little more. . . . Joanna, let your hand fall naturally from the wrist—and don't look so unhappy. . . . Cathy, you're getting better all the time."

The last twenty minutes were devoted to creative use of the combinations just learned. Starting in a corner, the children moved across the room, pretending to be flowers, lifting their arms like petals swaying in the breeze. When the lesson was over, Hannah ran through another, more advanced class with a group of eight- and nine-year-olds. At six o'clock it was time to go home.

Out on the street, the late-spring air was comfortably warm. Dressed in jeans and a blouse pulled over her leotard, she walked west toward the Seventh Avenue subway, oblivious to the admiring glances of men and women who passed by. At thirty-five, Hannah had aged well. Her body was firm, with every curve complementing her frame. Her face was warm, with a depth and maturity that made her every bit as attractive as in years gone by.

The ride to Broadway and 72nd Street, where she exited the subway, took twenty minutes. Before going home, she meandered through a recently opened boutique, then remembered she needed an ice cube tray and walked down the block to a hardware store just west of Columbus Avenue. Generally, hardware intimidated Hannah. Too much of it was difficult to describe, and she always felt awkward going into a store to ask for "one of those things you use to, whatever it is, you know what I mean." But an ice cube tray was easy.

The store owner was in his early forties, good-looking, slightly on the macho side with longish hair and a gold chain around his neck. For years, he'd flirted with her—and probably with every other attractive woman who came in—but always at a respectable distance, so Hannah still felt comfortable going in the store. The ice cube tray cost two dollars. She paid, dodged a young mother with a two-year-old in a stroller, and went back outside.

It was ten minutes to seven, or thereabouts. One of Hannah's eccentricities was that she never wore a watch yet was always on time. An internal clock of unknown origin woke her up each morning and saw her through each day. Another woman, this one with two children, passed by. She's got to be ten years younger than I am, Hannah told herself. Just for a moment, she thought ahead to the time when she'd be too old to have children. She wanted a child; at least she thought she did, but after what she'd gone through in childhood, she wasn't sure. And given the fact that she was between boyfriends with no marital prospects in sight—

"Watch it, lady!"

An out-of-control skateboarder whizzed by. Hannah kept walking until she reached West End Avenue, then turned south. She liked the neighborhood. Through seventeen years, four apartments, three roommates, and a marriage that failed, it had been her home. On 70th Street, just off West End Avenue, she came to the four-story brownstone where she lived alone. As with most New York residential buildings, the vestibule was bare except for an intercom and row of tiny metal mailboxes. Gathering her mail, she climbed the stairs to the third floor, unlocked the door to her apartment, and stepped inside.

Given the tight real estate market in Manhattan, the apartment was a gem. There was a bedroom, a walk-in kitchen, and a living room with a fireplace that worked. Also, if

Hannah stuck her head out the window, she could see the Hudson River. The furnishings were eclectic but well matched. Over the years, she'd frequented innumerable garage sales and flea markets, and having grown up surrounded by luxury, she had a good eye.

It was seven-twenty. A friend had promised to come by for a drink at eight o'clock. Crossing to the stereo, Hannah put on a recording of Mozart's Concerto No. 9 in E-flat Major, then went to the bathroom, turned on the bath water, and began to undress. Mozart had been twenty-one when he wrote the concerto; thirty-five (the same age as Hannah) when he died. When an artist dies young, she told herself, it's a tragedy; the whole world is deprived of his creations. Hannah wondered who, if anyone, would miss her when she died.

She was naked now, her jeans, shirt, leotard, and tights piled together on the floor. Returning to the living room, she turned the stereo volume up a notch so she could hear the harpsichord over the running water. The second movement of the concerto began.

"Oh, shit!"

Looking down, Hannah saw a cockroach wending its way across the floor. No matter how clean she kept her apartment, the roaches were always there. Slowly, she reached for a magazine, rolled it up, waited until the roach zigged when it should have zagged, and

33

brought her makeshift weapon crashing down. Congratulations, she told herself. You can outwit a cockroach.

Then she took her bath, dried herself, flipped Mozart over to the second side, and dressed. There was just enough time to check her mail—a catalogue from Saks, *The New Yorker*, a bill from American Express, and a letter, neatly addressed, with a West 88th Street return address on the outside. Opening the envelope, she began to read:

Dear Hannah:

I don't know if you remember me, but we went to high school together.

That was odd. Who? Looking ahead to the signature line, she saw the name Kyle Howard.

Kyle Howard. I remember Kyle! Bright, quiet, self-contained, shy. But why was Kyle writing now?

After college, I moved to New York and, not too long ago, I ran into Kathy Wilson (remember her?). She said you were living in the city. Given the fact that we're neighbors (I live on 88th Street between Columbus and Amsterdam), I thought it would be fun to get together and relive old times. A bit whimsical, but would you like to give it a try?

My telephone number is 875-0174. Feel free to call. If I don't hear from you, I'll give you a ring in the next week or so.

Best wishes,
Kyle Howard

Kyle Howard. Should she call? Probably not. Hannah wasn't sure she wanted to relive those particular memories. Besides, it felt funny getting a letter from someone she hadn't seen in—how long was it?—eighteen years. She and Kyle hadn't even been friends. Of course, outside of dancing, she hadn't had friends in high school, and not too many now.

Maybe it would be fun to get together, or at least interesting. Probably the thing to do was wait and see if Kyle called. Then, depending on how he sounded, she could make up her mind.

Hannah's internal clock struck eight P.M. Moments later, the doorbell rang.

Kyle Howard. I remember him.

□ □ □

Normally, Linda took the bus home from work, but the weather was nice and she'd decided to walk. Leaving her midtown office

35

behind, she started up Fifth Avenue, marveling at how the traffic thinned out after seven o'clock. Sidewalks that had been crammed with pedestrians an hour earlier were only sparsely populated. Cars flowed freely along the avenue. Stopping occasionally to window-shop, she made her way past St. Patrick's Cathedral, Trump Tower, Tiffany's, and a half-dozen more Manhattan landmarks. At 58th and Fifth, she came to the Plaza Hotel, stopped, and realized she was standing at the very spot where Robert Redford and Barbra Streisand had bade farewell to each other at the conclusion of *The Way We Were*. Then she saw the guy with the camera. Not bad-looking; slightly more than medium height; pleasant features. For a moment, Linda thought he was looking at her, but then she realized he was trying to take a picture of the Plaza Hotel and she was blocking his view.

"I'm sorry."

"No problem," he told her.

Moving aside, Linda watched as he pushed the shutter release button and advanced the film for his next shot. Then she started walking again, slowly so he could catch up because, on reflection, maybe he had been looking at her, and it was spring and it would be nice to have company walking home. On the corner of Fifth Avenue and 59th Street, he pulled even and they exchanged glances.

"Hi," he ventured.

Linda smiled.

"I know this sounds strange, but I've got one shot left on this roll of film. Could I take it of you?"

Very creative, Linda decided. A good opening line. And she was flattered because not too many people outside of family had ever asked to take her picture. Not that she was unattractive, but she wasn't a raving beauty either.

"Sure. Would you like it posed or my candid look?"

"Either way," he told her.

"How about candid?"

Backing off a few feet, he raised the camera to eye level and pressed the shutter release button. "Got ya," he said.

Then they began to walk again, exchanging biographical data along Central Park South.

She—Linda Taylor, twenty-five years old, born in Iowa; in New York for two years, working as a secretary for a travel agency, living in a one-bedroom apartment with a roommate who was on vacation in Europe. He—Arnold Tinsley, "a native New Yorker," which surprised Linda because it didn't sound as though he had a New York accent.

At Columbus Circle they turned north, making their way up Broadway to the mid-Seventies, where she stopped at a deli for a quart of milk. Arnold said he'd wait outside. "Fresh air," he told her. Linda thought maybe he was going to dump her and that was too bad because she kind of liked him, but when she came out of the deli he was still there. It was only then, after she'd bought the milk, that he asked if she wanted a drink and she did, but first she'd have to bring the milk upstairs to her apartment and put it in the refrigerator so it didn't spoil. He said no problem; he'd keep her company on the way up.

In the apartment, he asked for a glass of water and she gave it to him. Then she put the milk in the refrigerator, and when she returned to the living room, he was by the bookshelf looking at the books.

"Do you read a lot?"

"A little," she answered. "Most of the books belong to my roommate."

"What kind of books do you like to read?"

"Mysteries, thrillers. Anything with surprises and twists."

"How about life—do you like surprises in life?"

She was starting to get nervous. "I guess that depends. Surprises can be good or bad."

"This one is bad, Linda."

Chapter 3

IT WAS MIDMORNING. TWO PATROLMEN IN A SQUAD car were dispatched by 911. Richard Marritt was at his desk in the 20th Precinct stationhouse when their call came in. Linda Taylor, 259 West 76th Street, apartment 5-A. "It's a bad one," one of the patrolmen reported.

They're all bad, Marritt told himself as he made his way south to the victim's apartment. Except some homicides were worse than others, and when the detective arrived, he realized that the category this one fit into was the worst.

Linda Taylor had left work Tuesday around seven P.M. Several co-workers were worried when she didn't come in the next morning, but let the matter slide. Thursday, when she was still absent without calling in, the office manager sent a messenger to her apartment to ask the building superintendent if everything was all right. It wasn't.

Standing in the doorway, Marritt could see the body on the living room floor. The patrol-

men who answered the original call had
sealed off the apartment. Except for the
victim, there was no one inside. The furniture
was mostly secondhand, the rug a brown
artificial-fiber shag. The windows were open,
but there was no fire escape and no sign of
forced entry. There was no murder weapon in
sight.

The victim, in her mid-twenties, was fully
clothed, wearing a skirt, blouse, and sandals.
There was no indication that her undergar-
ments had been touched. A river of blood
traced from her neck. Shaken, the detective
began to make mental notes, matching the
scene with his police training. A person's
carotid arteries, he recalled, branch off the
aorta and run along either side of the neck.
They're protected by a tough sheath of muscle, and it takes a powerful direct knife thrust
to cut through. But once a carotid artery is
slashed, there's no way to survive; the victim
dies.

The room told the story. The moment
Linda Taylor's carotid artery had been severed, bright-red oxygenated blood began to
spurt, her life force pulsating onto the furniture and living room floor. Instinctively, she
had reached up with her left hand to close
the wound—thus the dried blood caked between her fingers—but the gesture was futile.
Within seconds, lack of oxygen to the brain
had caused her to faint. The blood continued

to spurt until her heart stopped beating. Within minutes she was dead, and a thin crust began to form, turning the bright red blood reddish-purple in hue.

Most likely, the victim hadn't resisted her killer. Faced with violence, the average person was passive. Few victims had the instinct to do what Marritt knew they should do. Explode. Smash an attacker flush on the nose; stick a finger through his eyeball into the brain.

Clinically, as unemotionally as possible, the detective continued his tour. The kitchen and bedroom seemed undisturbed. On the surface, at least, nothing had been stolen. The closets and drawers were all closed. In the bathroom, a bloody towel and bar of soap lay on the floor. Streaks of blood ran down the insides of the white porcelain sink. Probably the killer had washed his hands after the murder. There were no seminal stains on the rugs, bed, or victim's clothes; no traces of semen in the toilet. The killer hadn't sexually molested his victim. He'd "only" killed her.

For the next few hours, Marritt followed standard homicide procedure. Photographs were taken before the body was removed. The apartment was divided into a grid, and each section carefully searched by a team of police technicians utilizing vacuum equipment and infrared lights. Walls were checked from floor to ceiling. Fingerprints were taken from every possible source—doorknobs, the bathroom sink, an empty glass on the living room bookshelf.

By late afternoon the search was complete. There was still no way of knowing why Linda Taylor had been murdered. Of the almost two thousand homicides that occurred each year in the City of New York, most were instances where victims knew their attacker. Marritt hoped this was one of those instances, where the killer's name would show up in Linda Taylor's address book or on a list of friends. "Stranger murders" were the hardest to solve.

Something inside told the detective that this was a stranger murder—one that could give a headache to aspirin.

□ □ □ □

Hannah was in her bedroom when the telephone rang. Once. Twice. Reaching across the night table, she picked up the receiver on the third ring.

"Hello?"

"Hello. Is this Hannah?"

"Yes, it is."

"I don't know if you remember me. This is Kyle Howard."

Time for a decision, although Hannah had pretty much already made up her mind.

"Kyle—I got your letter. How are you?"

"Good. And you?"

"I'm fine."

There was a pause.

"I suppose it seemed strange hearing from me, but a few weeks ago I was thinking about high school. There were a few students I remembered well, and you were one of them. I thought I'd call to see if you'd like to get together for dinner sometime."

"All right."

"Great. What night is good for you?"

Turning to her datebook, Hannah did some quick calculating. Tonight was Thursday. Friday she was busy, and Saturday was too heavy-duty for this kind of date. Sunday didn't seem right. "How about Monday?"

"Fine. There's a restaurant called Sozio's on Columbus Avenue in the Eighties. Do you know it?"

"I think so. I've never been there, but I've passed by a couple of times."

"Let's meet there for dinner. What time is good for you?"

More calculating. Hannah finished teaching on Mondays at five-thirty. That meant she'd be home around six, bathed and dressed by seven. "How about eight?"

"Perfect. Would you like me to pick you up?"

"It's just as easy to meet at the restaurant."

"All right, I'll see you then. I'm looking forward to it."

The conversation done, Hannah hung up

43

the receiver, reflecting on the fact that she'd been seventeen years old when she'd last seen Kyle Howard. Time flew by.

She supposed she was looking forward to Monday night. Maybe reminiscing about old times would turn out to be fun. What concerned her more at the moment, though, was a package postmarked one day earlier. Like its predecessor, it had come in the mail wrapped in plain brown paper with no return address. Inside, again, were the headless stem and shriveled leaves of a long-stemmed rose and a crudely lettered two-by-three-inch card that read *THHIRWRDNK*.

Chapter 4

MONDAY EVENING: EIGHT O'CLOCK.

Hannah opened the door to Sozio's and stepped inside. The restaurant was one of many that had sprung up along Columbus Avenue in the 1980s. Some folded early; others flourished. Sozio's had been in business for three years—an indication that it would survive at least until its lease expired. Adjusting her eyes to the indoor light, Hannah looked past the maître d' to a row of chairs at the bar. Then she saw Kyle. He waved, came toward her, and they shook hands.

"Hannah, it's good to see you."

Eighteen years; that's how long it had been. He looked older, but otherwise pretty much the same. Six feet tall, maybe a shade shorter. Slender; not wiry or athletic, just thin. His features were ordinary, except for his mouth, which was a bit larger than it should have been. Hannah noted that his brown hair had begun to thin.

The maître d' led them to a table in back, and they sat facing each other. Kyle was wearing a brown suit, slightly frayed at the cuffs, striped shirt and tie. The restaurant was on the elegant side, with laser beam lights spotlighting lilies and orchids on each table.

"It's been a long time," Kyle said, beginning the conversation when they were seated. "What have you done since high school?"

It was the obvious first question, but capsulizing eighteen years into a one-paragraph answer wasn't the easiest task to perform. What should I say, Hannah wondered. I've danced, been married, gotten a divorce, taught.

"Right after I graduated, I came to New York," she answered. "I don't know if you remember, but I danced a lot in high school, and summers I was usually out of town—studying in Chicago after eleventh grade, ballet camp before then. In New York, I danced with the American Ballet Theatre for four years. Then I developed back trouble. I've been teaching ballet to children since then."

A waiter came by, handed them menus, and took their drink orders. It seemed to Hannah that Kyle was a bit nervous.

"What about you?" she asked. "What have you done since high school?"

"Nothing terribly exciting. I went to college at Williams. Then I came to New York

46

and taught high school English for a while, but it wasn't what I wanted to do. What I really wanted was to be a writer."

Fragments from the past were beginning to fall into place. She remembered now; Kyle had always wanted to be a writer. He was the one who had read Dickens in high school. Not just *A Tale of Two Cities*, which they made you read in eleventh grade, but *Great Expectations*, *Bleak House*, and *Nicholas Nickleby*. His family had lived in Toledo or someplace like that, and moved to Davis after his sophomore year. That meant he'd only had two years to make friends in high school. Davis had been cliquish; Kyle had been quiet and shy.

"Have you been married?" she heard Kyle asking.

"A long time ago. It wasn't exactly a marriage made in heaven."

"Any prospects on the horizon?"

"Not at the moment. I'm woefully available."

The waiter returned with their drinks, and suggested they review the menu so he could take their order. Everything was à la carte. Despite Kyle's urging, Hannah passed on the appetizer.

"What did your husband do for a living?" he queried after they'd chosen entrees.

"He was an investment banker."

"How long were you married?"

"Ten months. But what about you? Have you been married?"

He shook his head. "I've had the normal complement of friends and lovers, but no one I wanted to spend the rest of my life with."

"How long did you teach high school?"

"Two years. It was all right, but it wasn't something I wanted to do."

"And your writing?"

"I've mixed it in with other jobs."

The dialogue continued, focusing mostly on get-acquainted conversation. Then they turned to high school nostalgia. "I saw Ellis Barnes about five years ago," Hannah offered. "He weighs three hundred pounds and looks like Orson Welles. I can't believe we went to high school with someone who looks like Orson Welles."

"And Mr. Lundahl, the math teacher. Do you remember him? He actually fell asleep in class one time."

The entrees arrived—elaborate pasta for both of them. A little overcooked, but more than passable. As they began to eat, Hannah evaluated her dinner companion. There was no physical attraction, but Kyle did have a certain charm about him. His voice was expressive. He was articulate and well read.

"You still haven't told me; what have you written?"

"Articles," he answered. "Although I haven't done many lately. And I've written a novel."

48

"Kyle, that's wonderful. What's it about?"

"The usual—life, love, the great American novel."

Then, again, he shifted the conversation back to growing up in Ohio—walking to school on the road by the brook; football games that Hannah never attended. Next came family. "My father was a foreman in a glass factory," he told her. "My mother taught fourth grade. When my father died a few years ago, my mother retired and moved to Florida."

"Have you been in touch with anyone from Davis?"

"Not lately."

"Except Kathy Wilson," she prodded. "You mentioned her in your letter. Where did you see Kathy?"

"At Omnibus."

"What's Omnibus?"

"The bookstore where I work." His voice took on a tone that seemed midway between resentment and confession. "It's not the career of my dreams, but it pays the bills. I'm a salesman and order clerk."

She had to ask, if for no other reason than to eliminate the awkwardness she felt growing between them.

"And your novel?"

"It fits into the category publishers refer to as 'literary fiction.' That means they don't think they can sell many copies unless I

49

change the book to make it more commercial, and I won't do that. I'll show it to you sometime if you'd like."

"I'd like that very much."

For the rest of the meal they stayed with nostalgia. Basically, Hannah felt sorry for him. All his life, Kyle had wanted to be a writer and, so far at least, he'd failed. At thirty-five he was unpublished, working at a job he seemed to dislike, very far from fulfillment of his goals. Also, it occurred to her that the restaurant was relatively nice, dinner for two would cost at least fifty dollars, and it was unlikely that salesmen at Omnibus got paid top dollar. When the check came, she offered to pay half, but Kyle resisted. "That's not fair; I invited you. You can buy me an ice-cream cone sometime."

After dinner he walked her home. Whatever the reason, he seemed more comfortable, as though the outdoor air helped him relax and let off nervous energy. When they reached her apartment, Hannah considered thanking him for dinner and saying good night, but good manners dictated inviting him upstairs for coffee. She was neither pleased nor displeased when he accepted. In her apartment, Kyle opened up a little more about his job and his writing, and she wondered which was worse— knowing you were good but having your career cut short (as hers was) or never knowing if you were good at all. At eleven o'clock he said it was getting late. She concurred, and rose to walk him to the door. Except he didn't follow. Instead, he stayed by the sofa, averting his eyes from hers.

"I suppose . . . I suppose I should tell you why I called."

"I don't understand. I thought you called to catch up on old times." Hannah's voice trailed off, and she waited for him to speak again.

"I . . . I'm not sure how to say this . . ." His hands were busy, fingers twisting and interlocking with one another. "Hannah, for twenty years, ever since I first saw you in high school, I've been in love with you." The words came slowly, like a 45 record played at 33 rpm speed. "Hannah, I'm obsessed with you. I think about you all the time. I dream about you constantly. I love you. I'm not asking for anything from you. I just wanted you to know."

Then there was silence as Hannah sucked in air, telling herself that this was Looney Tunes.

"Kyle, I don't know what to say. I mean, I'm flattered, but I don't feel that way about you."

All she really wanted was to get him out of the apartment. She was closer to the door than he was. She could run if she had to.

"I. . . . Sure, I understand . . . I just wanted you to know . . . I mean—"

How can you love me? Hannah wanted to shout. You don't even know me.

Again, she heard Kyle talking.

"Sometimes it takes a long time to say things that are important. I. . . . Maybe I could call again, and we could have lunch together sometime next week."

Just get him out. Get him out of the apartment.

"That would be nice. Call me and we'll talk about it."

She hadn't wanted to say "that would be nice," but she was afraid her answer would antagonize him without it.

"All right, I'll call. And I enjoyed seeing you tonight—really."

He was leaving. He was coming toward her . . . past her . . . to the door.

"It was nice to see you, too, Kyle."

Thank God. He wasn't going to try to kiss her.

Hannah opened the door.

Kyle stopped. "Well, okay. I'll call sometime next week. Have a good night."

And then he was gone.

Hannah closed the door, locked both locks, and listened to his footsteps on the stairs. Then she went to the window and, with the living room light out so he couldn't see her, watched as he left the building and disappeared down the street.

Oh, God! What have I gotten into? Calm

down; don't overreact. Maybe she was blowing the whole thing out of proportion. After all, Kyle hadn't done anything. Not tonight. Not for eighteen years.

Back to the bedroom. The fear was still there; it wasn't subsiding. Eighteen years! Why now?

Hannah felt trapped. She didn't know what to do. She needed help, someone to lean on. So she did what she always did when she felt nervous or vulnerable or lonely or scared.

She picked up the telephone and called Fergy.

PART TWO

PART TWO

Chapter 5

STEPHEN ANDREW FERGENSON—"FERGY" TO HIS friends—was born in Minnesota near the Canadian border. His mother was a waitress who found herself pregnant at age seventeen. What Missy Fergenson really wanted was an abortion, but she got married instead. Two years after Fergy was born, the marriage ended. Three years later, Missy Fergenson tried again, this time reversing the order of things—first the ceremony, then the pregnancy. Marriage number two lasted seven months; the pregnancy, five. This time there was an abortion, followed by another abortion two years later. "I was afraid she'd get rid of me if I wasn't good," Fergy later recalled. "When prospective babies kept disappearing, it made me think that I was expendable too."

Still, Missy tried hard to be a good mother. She moved to Detroit, took a job as a secretary, put Fergy through school, and gave him "lots of love." Neither of her former husbands contributed financially, emotionally, or any other way, so life was hard, but she must have done something right, because Fergy turned out to be a joy. And when he finished graduate school, tenth in his class with an M.B.A. from the University of Michigan, Missy was justifiably proud. Her "little mistake" had become a man.

After graduation, Fergy came to New York and took a job with Peterson Brownfield & Company. He lasted on Wall Street for nine years. He was good, but not a star. He liked his work, but not a lot. By age thirty-four he was sufficiently bored that he left investment banking for the public sector, more specifically the New York City Public Development Corporation, an agency devoted to various urban renewal projects. Two months after the start of his career as a public servant, Fergy was called for jury duty, which he hated—until he met Hannah, who had also been called. Then, suddenly, jury duty was pure bliss. Instead of sitting around for eight hours a day reading magazines and waiting to be picked for a jury, Fergy was sitting around for eight hours a day hoping he wouldn't be picked, because that would separate him from the woman of his dreams.

Hannah liked Fergy. They identified with one another, and shared the common bond of coming from a broken home. In the confines of the jury room, they became friends. From Hannah's point of view, there wasn't really a physical attraction. Fergy was nice enough looking, she supposed, but he was pudgy. He watched his weight; he just couldn't help it. That's the way his body was. They were quasi-neighbors, it turned out, Fergy living on 21st Street between Eighth and Ninth avenues. When their jury duty ended, they stayed friends. Two years had passed since then, and during that time, they'd come to rely on each other. Fergy was Hannah's stabilizing force, her Rock of Gibraltar. Whenever she was down, he was available. If she was sick and needed tetracycline, somehow Fergy could get it without a prescription. When she was suffering from nicotine withdrawal in the midst of an all-out effort to give up smoking, Fergy was there ("We're going out for a very expensive dinner, Hannah. If you do not have a cigarette, I will treat you. If you do have a cigarette, you will treat me.") And the friendship worked both ways. Hannah was someone Fergy could open up to. Whatever was on his mind, whatever troubled him, she wanted to hear. If Fergy was having woman problems, Hannah listened. If a huge black cloud hung over his life every day because he was thirty-six and lonely, she could understand. In truth, they were both a little afraid that life might pass them by. And they'd learned that it was possible to get close to each other not only by reaching out to help, but also by reaching out to ask for help in return.

Kyle Howard left Hannah's apartment at eleven-fifteen. By eleven-forty—twenty minutes after her call—Fergy was there. Hannah could count on him for things like that, always.

"Thanks for coming."

"My pleasure," he told her. "When you called, I was trying to decide whether to watch television or go to bed. Coming here seemed far more interesting." He paused, as though an interval of several seconds was necessary before coming to the business at hand. "All right, Hannah Banana. What's the story?"

She smiled—Fergy had a way of making her do that—and relaxed a bit. "It's weird."

"It certainly sounded that way on the telephone. Suppose we start at square one."

She began with Kyle's letter, then his telephone call, followed by dinner and the conversation in her apartment afterward. Fergy listened with a mixture of concern and bemusement. Concern because Hannah was upset and, probably, the whole thing had been pretty scary. Bemusement because Kyle was obviously a nut, and if you looked at it in a certain light, what was scary turned funny.

"I guess the important thing is not to let your imagination run away with you," he said when she'd finished. "Most likely, he's harmless."

"Thanks a lot."

"You're welcome. Now, calm down and look at it objectively for a moment. You're beautiful, you're wonderful, you're sexy, you're smart. Like Kyle said, he's had a thing for you since high school. Probably, as tonight wore on, he realized you weren't responding, so he decided to go out in a blaze of glory."

"Does that mean he's gone for good?"

"I don't know. He'll probably call next week like he said he would. Tell him no, and that'll be the end of it."

Trying his best to reassure her, Fergy smiled.

"Oh, shit," Hannah blurted out. "The roses."

"What roses?"

"The roses, the ones I told you about. Two months ago, in April, remember? I got a rose in the mail with the head cut off and that card. And last Thursday, the day Kyle called, there was another one. Kyle must have sent them."

"Why?"

"I don't know why. Because he's a psycho."

"I guess you're not going to fall in love with this guy, are you?"

Hannah laughed. She didn't know why; she just had to.

Mission accomplished, Fergy turned more

serious. "The roses. What did you do with them?"

"I threw them out. Why?"

"I don't know. I just thought maybe there was something we could learn from them."

"But I kept the card—not the first one, but the second."

"Could I see it?"

"Sure." Leaving Fergy behind, Hannah went into the bedroom, rummaged through her desk, and returned triumphant a minute later. "Here."

Fergy took the card, and stared at the simple block letters—*THHIRWRDNK*.

"What do you think it means?" she queried.

"I don't know. Maybe it's a provincial capital in northern Thailand . . . Thir-ridink . . . Thir—I can't pronounce it. It needs more vowels. Ask Kyle the next time he calls."

"Thanks, but I'd rather keep the conversation to a minimum."

"Maybe it has something to do with high school. The initials of a teacher or school organization."

"With ten letters?"

"Don't be critical. It's just a thought." Again, Fergy studied the card. "You don't still have your high school yearbook, do you?"

"What good would that do?"

"I don't know. Maybe there's some kind of

clue in it. Besides, I'm curious to see what Kyle looked like in high school."

"Fergy, I love you, but sometimes you're a pain in the ass."

"Thank you. Now, where's the yearbook?"

"In the bedroom closet, I think. Unless I threw it out years ago."

Grumbling, Hannah rose from the sofa and disappeared into the bedroom. Fergy heard the closet door open. There was a loud "oh, shit" followed by what sounded like a box falling to the floor. Then she returned, yearbook in hand. "Here."

"Fantastic." Reaching for the yearbook, Fergy glanced at the cover, then opened it up and turned to page one. There was the obligatory photo of Davis High School, followed on succeeding pages by faculty members, varsity teams, extracurricular activity groups, and underclassmen. Toward the end of the book, he came to the senior class photos— Vaughan . . . Volk . . . Wade: Hannah Wade. With Hannah looking over his shoulder, he stared at the portrait of a seventeen-year-old girl wearing a white sweater with a single strand of pearls. "God, you were beautiful."

"Fergy, we're supposed to be looking for Kyle."

Shrugging, Fergy flipped back a few pages. Haley . . . Hess. . . .

"Here he is—Kyle Howard." Wordlessly, they stared at the photo. Like the other male students, Kyle was wearing a white shirt, dark sports jacket, and tie. His expression was serious, his hair a bit shorter than average. Nothing in the photo suggested anything extraordinary. "Kyle transferred to Davis at the start of his junior year," read the caption. "An avid reader, he's interested in classical music and is a member of the Latin Honor Society."

"Any clues?" Hannah prodded.

Fergy shook his head. "How come there aren't any autographs? When I went to high school, at the end of the year everyone ran around with their yearbook, collecting autographs."

"I don't know. I guess I didn't care one way or the other."

"Did Kyle ask you to autograph his yearbook?"

"Jerk. You're talking about something that happened, or didn't happen, eighteen years ago."

"Okay, don't get touchy." Again, Fergy studied the photo of Kyle. "Who did this guy hang out with in high school?"

Hannah furrowed her brow. "I don't remember. I mean, I didn't know Kyle well. I never saw him with anyone."

Shaking his head again, Fergy closed the yearbook. "I don't know. I guess we all have strange memories of high school. I still remember my first date, high school dances, all those things. Kyle just happens to be a little weirder than the rest of us. That's all. Don't worry about him." Wearily, he glanced at his watch, then stood up. "Listen, Hannah Banana. It's one o'clock, and some of us have to go to work in the morning. In eight hours I'm supposed to present a funding proposal for an industrial park in the South Bronx."

Hannah kissed him on the cheek, then gave him a hug. "Be careful going home, Fergy, and thanks for coming."

"My pleasure. Now get some sleep."

Fergy left. Hannah locked the door behind him, then went back to the living room and picked up the yearbook. She didn't like what was happening. Something inside told her to watch out. Maybe she was psychic. From time to time, she'd had feelings, she thought— her mind broke off. She didn't want to develop that part of her. Thumbing through the yearbook again, Hannah returned to Kyle's photo: "An avid reader, he's interested in classical music and is a member of the Latin Honor Society." Hannah had endured three years of Latin. Her grandparents had made her take it. She'd been a member of the Latin Honor Society too.

Turning to the extracurricular activities section, she scanned the pages: Student Government . . . Glee Club . . . Library Committee . . . Red Cross. . . .

Latin Honor Society. There were twenty

students sitting in the gymnasium bleachers. Mr. Rouse, the Latin teacher, sat in the first row. Hannah was in row two of the photo. Nineteen students and Mr. Rouse were facing the photographer, smiling into the camera. Kyle sat in the third row, one row behind Hannah, one person to the side. His face was unsmiling. He was staring at her.

Chapter 6

ONE WEEK HAD PASSED SINCE LINDA TAYLOR'S murder; five days since her body had been discovered. Richard Marritt sat at his desk on the second floor of the 20th Precinct stationhouse, wrestling with the intricacies of changing a typewriter ribbon. His back ached—the result of scaling an eight-foot-high wall in pursuit of a killer the previous autumn. For his efforts, the detective had gotten his man, been awarded a departmental merit citation, and twisted his back in a way that led to periodic muscle spasms. Sometimes now, when the back acted up, he wondered what it would be like to work on a suburban police force, where a typical investigation centered on who had left car tire tracks on someone else's front lawn.

The door to the office opened, and Jim Dema entered. Two years of working together had fine-tuned the relationship between them. Marritt had even stopped worrying that people would think he was gay simply because he had a gay partner. Looking up from his typewriter, the detective nodded hello, then went back to changing the ribbon. Dema took a seat opposite the desk and, as always, waited for Marritt to begin the conversation.

"David is acting up again," the detective said. "Eight years old, and he thinks he's deprived because we don't have cable TV. Last night I thought I'd teach him to whittle. Nobody does it anymore, but I figured it would be more creative than watching *Conan the Barbarian*."

"And?"

"David wanted to go next door to watch *Conan the Barbarian*, but my wife said he couldn't until he cleaned up his room, which resembles Death Valley at the moment. David threw a fit. Then Jonathan got into the act by spilling David's soap bubble mix on the living room sofa. David started yelling at Jonathan; Jonathan yelled back. My wife screamed at Jonathan to clean up the bubble mix. David complained about getting less parental attention than Jonathan; Jonathan complained about getting less parental attention than David. I figure if they both feel that way, I can rest easy that they're being equally treated." Marritt finished inserting the typewriter ribbon, licked his smudged fingertips, and wiped them on his trousers. "Anyway, that's what's happening at home. I suppose we've got more important things to talk about here at the office. Have the lab reports come in on Linda Taylor?"

Dema nodded. "We're in good shape if we find a suspect. The fingerprints from the bathroom sink match up with the glass you found on the living room bookshelf. The blood on the towel was Linda Taylor's, but the hair on the towel came from someone else—a white male, according to the lab report."

"What about the autopsy?"

"Nothing. No drugs; no liquor; no beating or sexual molestation. Just one simple thrust through the carotid artery. The wound indicates that the killer was right-handed."

Marritt stared down at a stack of reports lying on his desk. Several hours after Linda Taylor's body had been discovered, a half-dozen detectives had gone to work. Friends, neighbors, co-workers, and relatives had been interviewed. Everyone whose name appeared in the victim's address book had been contacted. Nothing out of the ordinary had been discovered. One of the things Marritt disliked about murder investigations was that invariably they wound up violating the victim's privacy. Secret sexual liaisons, financial problems, and other embarrassing details were often uncovered. But with Linda Taylor, nothing so far seemed out of the ordinary. There was an average family, an average job, an average apartment, average friends. She'd left work at seven o'clock one night, and been stabbed to death hours later.

"Probably, she let the perpetrator into her apartment," the detective said, looking toward Dema. "As for why she let him in, that's anyone's guess. Maybe he knocked on the door and said he was a neighbor. Maybe it was an old boyfriend she'd known for years. If the fingerprints on the glass belong to the killer, the odds are he was there socially." Marritt's frustration was evident as he talked. "But on the other hand, for all we know he killed her and then helped himself to a glass of water."

"Would that make sense?"

"For a killer? Sure, anything makes sense. He washed his hands, didn't he? Why not take a glass of water? If you're talking about common sense, why do people let other people they don't know into their apartment? Why do women who wouldn't talk to a stranger on the street sign petitions to stop nuclear testing or save the whales, and write their name and address on the petition so any nut who collects petitions can look them up in the phone book, make obscene telephone calls, or follow them home?"

Opening a folder beneath his reports, the detective scanned a series of newspaper clippings. *The New York Times* had given the murder only cursory coverage. The *Daily News* and *Post* were more voluble, with the *Post* playing up the "she was a sweet girl" angle. At the end of the *Post* story, anyone with information was asked to call the police at 520-9200.

"Have there been any tips?" the detective queried.

"None that checked out."

"What about the funeral?"

"We had it covered and took photographs of everyone who attended."

Marritt turned to another folder, one with photographs of the murder site. Nothing seemed out of the ordinary except the body. "There's no guarantee that the fingerprints belong to the killer," he said at last. "But right now, it's a good guess. I suppose we just have to keep interviewing. One friend will lead to another, who will lead to a third, who will lead to a fourth. But I've got a feeling it won't help. The whole thing is too antiseptic to have been done by an acquaintance."

"Antiseptic?"

"That's what I said. How many murders have you seen where the victim was stabbed once and the one thrust was as professional as this? When did you see a case where the victim was killed this efficiently, and then the perpetrator left fingerprints all over the place?" Marritt paused, gathering his thoughts. "What I'm saying is, this wasn't an un-planned killing—a burglar who was interrupted

71

or a crime of passion in the traditional sense. Someone went to Linda Taylor's apartment for the purpose of killing her, someone who was very good at it."

Chapter 7

FOR HANNAH, THE DAYS AFTER HER ENCOUNTER with Kyle offered little out of the ordinary. She taught, took walks, read, did what she normally did with her spare time. On occasion she thought back to high school, but each time she broke off. After eighteen years of shutting out memories, she was determined not to relive the past now. Over the weekend she took in a concert, had a blind date, and went out for pizza with Fergy. Monday afternoon she was back in class, teaching again.

"All right, Diana. Stand up straight. First position. Heels together with your toes pointed in the opposite direction. Put your feet in a straight line. . . . That's it. Keep your knees together. It doesn't count if your knees are apart."

After class she took the subway home, where there was "an automatic oh fuck" as she entered the apartment. ("An automatic oh fuck," Fergy once explained to her, "is

73

when you flick the switch to turn on a light, the bulb pops, and you say, 'Oh, fuck.' ")

Hannah changed the light bulb, took a bath, and made dinner. At nine o'clock sharp, the telephone rang.

"Hi, it's Kyle Howard. How are you?"

Something inside her seemed to drop. She'd known he'd call, but not really. In her heart she'd expected it, but intellectually she'd chosen not to prepare for the moment.

"I'm fine, Kyle. How are you?"

"I'm good." There was a long pause. "How has your week been?"

"Fine. And yours?'

"I've had a good week, really good." Another pause. "I called to see if you'd like to have lunch tomorrow."

"I appreciate the invitation, but tomorrow I'm busy."

"How about Wednesday?'

"That's not good either."

"Okay ... I guess. ... There's a three-day weekend coming up. I could rent a car, and maybe we could spend a day at the beach together."

The irony of it was, Hannah had no plans for the Fourth of July weekend.

"Kyle, I just don't think it's a good idea. I was delighted to exchange memories with you, but I really don't think it would be good for either of us to pursue this further."

"Well, sure. I mean, I understand, but couldn't I see you just once?"

"We've already seen each other. Why prolong what doesn't work?"

"I'm not sure I understand."

"Kyle, it's very simple. I don't want to belittle what you told me the other night. I'm sure it came from the heart, but I don't share your feelings. I'm not the person you think I am, and in light of what was said, I really wouldn't feel comfortable being with you."

"Sure, I mean about some things maybe you're right. I was thinking about the past week too. I think a lot of it had to do with memories. But it would help . . . seeing you just once more would help me get over it. That would be all right, wouldn't it?"

"Would what be all right?"

"Seeing each other just once more—for lunch or a walk. That way, it would be easier for me to put things in perspective."

Hannah felt her resolve weakening; why, she wasn't sure.

"Kyle, I don't know."

"Please! Just a walk in the park. It would make it easier for me to deal with the situation."

She couldn't believe it. He was actually pleading.

"We could take a walk and—"

"All right," Hannah told him. "A walk. But,

Kyle, I don't want to give you any false hope."

"Sure. I mean, that's fine." The desperation in his voice seemed to ease just a bit. "When would be best for you to do it?"

"Thursday. I'll meet you at Columbus Circle at two o'clock."

It was inevitable, of course—it rained on Thursday. Hannah thought about simply not showing up, leaving Kyle standing alone in the rain, but she was too responsible to do that. Then she considered calling to change the time or place, but she didn't want to dial his telephone number. At two o'clock, as scheduled, she arrived at Columbus Circle. Kyle was standing at the northeast corner of the intersection, wearing brown slacks, a white shirt, and rubbers. Hannah couldn't remember the last time she'd been with a contemporary who was wearing rubbers. He waved. They drew toward each other, umbrellas overhead to ward off the rain.

"I guess it's not very good weather for a walk," he said, beginning the conversation. "Why don't we find someplace nearby for a cup of coffee?"

Hannah nodded in acquiescence and they began to walk north, coming to a delicatessen several blocks away on Broadway. Inside, they took seats at a booth. Kyle ordered a piece of blueberry pie; Hannah, a Coke.

"Are you sure you don't want something to eat?"

"I have a class to teach at three-thirty," she answered.

Good move, Hannah told herself. Now she was on record with an excuse for leaving at three o'clock.

"I saw the Jackson Pollack exhibit at the Museum of Modern Art," Kyle said, turning to a more substantive topic. "Do you like his work?"

"Not much. He's always struck me as somewhat repetitious."

"I guess that's right. I don't like him much either. Which painters do you like?"

"From Pollack's generation, Paul Klee, Chagall, and Edward Hopper."

It was an inane conversation. At the moment, neither of them had the slightest interest in talking about painting.

"When I was a kid," Kyle told her, "I saw a print of El Greco's *View of Toledo* in a book about sixteenth-century art. For years, I thought it was supposed to be a painting of Toledo, Ohio."

Hannah forced a smile, and offered thanks for the arrival of her Coke. The straw would give her something to fidget with while they talked.

"Do you go to museums a lot?"

"I try to," she answered.

Her internal clock read two-twenty. She

wondered what Kyle was trying to accomplish by this meeting. Forty minutes to go. The conversation moved from art to theater to Elizabethan literature, as though Kyle had come armed with a list of topics so there'd be no awkward gaps or silent moments. It's hopeless, she wanted to tell him. Don't try to make me feel something I don't; it won't work. But he seemed content to avoid the subject of his obsession, and it was his show. He'd requested this one last encounter.

Two-thirty.... Two thirty-two.... Hannah glanced down at Kyle's watch to confirm her internal chronometer. She'd never known time to move so slowly.

"Do you have any plans for the holiday weekend?"

"I'm spending it with friends," she answered.

Two thirty-four.... Two thirty-five.... The conversation turned to high school; terrain they'd covered on their previous "date." "I guess I wasn't very popular back then," Kyle acknowledged. "When people had parties, I wasn't invited. Mostly, I had books and television instead of friends." He seemed on the verge of going further, then drew back.

Two thirty-nine.... Two-forty. There wasn't much point in prolonging the agony by waiting until three o'clock. Hannah opened her pocketbook and reached for her purse.

"Kyle, I've got to go. I have a class I can't be late for."

"Let me treat."

"That's all right. I'll pay for my own Coke."
Probably, she should pay for his blueberry
pie; he had treated her to dinner their last
time out. But she didn't want to offer any
encouragement.

"Okay, well. . . . It was nice to see you."

Hannah stood up. "I hope you have a good
day, Kyle."

"Sure, you too. . . . I. . . . Maybe we could
get together again sometime next week."

Maybe the best thing would be to just not
answer.

"Would that be possible?"

"Kyle, I don't think so."

"Why not?"

Part of Hannah wanted to reach out and
shake him by the neck.

"Kyle, I've told you before how I feel about
this. You said you wanted to get together one
last time and I accepted, but that's it."

"I don't understand. I mean, I'm perfectly
willing to see each other as friends."

Hannah took a deep breath. "That's not
how life works. I wouldn't be comfortable,
and it isn't what you want. Besides, I'm not
the person you think I am. Even if we spent
time together, you wouldn't be happy."

"That's possible. But it's also possible that,
if we spent time together, you might feel
differently about me."

Hannah felt herself getting angry. "Look,

Kyle, thinking this way isn't healthy. Other people have had crushes and gone on with their life."

"Okay. I mean, why don't we do this. You think about it, and I'll call sometime next week."

"I'd rather you didn't. I have your number. If I change my mind, I'll call. But I'm telling you now, I'm sure I won't."

Hannah's head was starting to hurt, her blood vessels dilating to stretch the surrounding connective tissue. Get away from me, she wanted to shout. Leave me alone.

"All right. Well, if you change your mind, I'll be around all next week."

Maybe there was time to go home before class for some Cafergot to stave off the pain of her oncoming migraine headache. Kyle was staring at her as if she were some kind of mythic goddess. What time was it? A little before three o'clock. Class was at three-thirty. Probably she could go home first and still make it.

"Kyle, I'll be late for class. I've got to go now. Good-bye."

"You're my Catherine. Do you know that?"

"What?"

"I feel like Heathcliff, and you're my Catherine. *Wuthering Heights*. They loved each other even though they were apart for years."

Before Hannah knew it, her response tumbled out. "Yes, Kyle. I read the book, and

saw the movie. But you're not Laurence
Olivier, and you're leaving out one other
detail. Heathcliff and Catherine were lovers;
they had a relationship before they were apart."

□ □ □

The main reading room at the New York
City Public Library was surprisingly comfortable. Two dozen long wood-grained tables
provided ample space to work. The forty-foot
ceiling and eight brass chandeliers added a
touch of elegance to the surroundings.

It was five-thirty. Alison Schoenfeld stared
at the papers spread out in front of her and
rubbed her eyes. The library was closing in
thirty minutes. She'd been working on her
dissertation for two years; quitting a half
hour early wouldn't hamper her progress.
Opening her attaché case, she began to gather
her papers preparatory to leaving. Then she
noticed the man standing at the adjacent
table. He was an inch or two shy of six feet,
in his mid-thirties with brown hair; pleasant-
looking. For a moment, she thought he'd been
looking at her. He tucked his folio under his
arm and started toward the door. Then Alison
noticed that his wallet was sticking out of his
hip pocket, as though a pickpocket had tried to
lift it and came close but failed. Suddenly, as
if on cue, the wallet slid the rest of the way
out of his pocket and tumbled to the floor.

"Excuse me," Alison called out.

The guy didn't seem to hear. He kept walking.

"Excuse me."

It still wasn't loud enough to get his attention. And this was a library; she didn't feel like shouting. So Alison walked over, scooped up the wallet, and caught up to him at the door.

"Excuse me. I think you dropped this when you were leaving."

Instinctively, he reached for his back pocket.

"Oh, my God! Thank you."

Alison handed him the wallet.

"Thank you," he repeated, shaking his head. "That's never happened to me before."

They moved past the security guard, down two flights of marble stairs to the Fifth Avenue revolving door. "I can't tell you how much I appreciate that," he said as they walked. "You hear all sorts of awful stories about New York and New Yorkers, but thanks to you, my faith is restored."

Outside, it was raining. As they exited onto Fifth Avenue, he drew closer and opened his umbrella. "Could I walk you someplace? The least I can do is protect you against the elements."

Why not, Alison decided. Half an umbrella was better than none in the rain.

"I live in the Twenties, between Park Avenue South and Madison," she told him. "If that's out of the way, a bus stop would be fine."

"Not at all. I'd be delighted to walk you home. My name is Arnold Tinsley."

"I'm Alison."

"What were you working on in the library?"

"My dissertation." She wasn't in the habit of talking with strangers, but Arnold seemed fairly nice. Also, it wasn't as though he had sought her out. A dropped wallet had brought them together. But she was worried he'd think she was a professional student, and at age thirty-two that wasn't so good, so she added, "I'm a doctoral candidate at NYU; it's only part-time. The rest of the time, I'm a social worker."

Much to her surprise, he professed interest in her job. Most people were bored by social work; it was nice to find someone who seemed to care. The rain poured down; Alison was thankful for her half of the umbrella. At 29th Street and Fifth Avenue, she pointed east. "I live down there."

Arnold looked ahead to the corner of 28th Street, a block further on. For a moment, Alison thought he hadn't heard her. "Turn left," she started to say.

"One more block," he told her.

"But I live down here, on Twenty-ninth Street."

"I know. But walk with me just one block more."

"Why?"

"You'll see."

Alison shrugged. He had the umbrella. There probably wasn't any harm in—

Then she saw why they were walking the extra block. Standing on the corner of Fifth Avenue and 28th Street, there was a solitary vendor selling long-stemmed roses in the rain. When they reached the corner, Arnold handed the vendor a dollar, took a rose, and with a grand flourish, presented it to Alison. "To my savior. Without you, I'd have no money to buy this rose."

"Arnold, you're wonderful."

"Thank you."

She had no plans for the evening. It wasn't every day that a stranger bought her a long-stemmed rose. They walked the one block back up Fifth Avenue, then east along 29th Street to the stoop of the brownstone where Alison lived. It was now or never. Invite him up or never see him again.

"Would you like to come up for a cup of coffee?"

"I'd be delighted," he told her.

He really was. It gave him confidence when the woman made the first move.

Chapter 8

THE SUN CAME BACK ON THE FOURTH OF JULY. Perfect beach weather, except there was no beach. Hannah slept late and fixed a light brunch before meeting Fergy for a walk in Central Park.

"It was a long night last night," he announced as they reached the Strawberry Fields section of the park at 72nd Street.

"How come?"

"A blind date. When I got to her apartment, the door was open and she was sitting on the floor in some sort of yoga position, releasing tension or causing tension; I'm not sure which."

A blaring cassette player interrupted his report.

"Anyway," he continued, "I had to sit without talking for ten minutes while she finished her mantra. Then we went out for dinner, and she talked exclusively about Pac-Man, astrological signs, and Madonna. Afterward, she invited me back to her apartment and I went; why, I'm not sure. I guess it was because she had blond hair. I felt lucky, and I've never had much luck with blondes. We kissed once or twice, and then she bit my tongue."

"She what?"

"Bit my tongue. It hurt like hell. After I stopped shouting, she told me she was into kinky sex and I could do anything I wanted. I thought about it, and decided that what I wanted to do more than anything else in the world was leave, so I left." Stopping for a moment, he turned toward Hannah and stuck out his tongue. "See? That little red mark? She did that."

Hannah examined the wound, and Fergy returned his tongue to its proper place. Then they continued walking, past Bethesda Fountain toward the boathouse by the lake. The park was crowded with afternoon picnickers, bike riders, and sun worshippers. Why do you go out with these women? Hannah wanted to ask; because the truth of it was, Fergy was always going out with dingbats and women he slept with once and never saw again. But she didn't ask, because this one had been a blind date, and the fact of the matter was, she'd just been out with an even bigger dingbat.

"I saw Kyle Howard yesterday," Hannah confessed as they reached the boathouse.

"You what?"

"I saw Kyle—for coffee before class."

"Why?"

"I don't know. He called. He pleaded and begged. All he wanted was to take a walk. What can I say? I guess I'm a softie."

"Obviously. But when you get an obscene phone call, you're supposed to hang up."

"I thought about asking if he sent the roses," Hannah said, shifting gears somewhat. "Then I decided it was pointless because he'd just deny it. Look, seeing him was stupid but it's already done, so why don't we talk about something else."

They came to a vendor who was selling DoveBars. Deciding she was hungry, Hannah announced it was her treat. They both chose vanilla. She paid; then they walked to the shade of a tree and sat on the grass facing each other.

"Do you ever miss Wall Street?" she asked, reaffirming her intention to change the subject.

"Not really," Fergy answered. "Sometimes I look at my paycheck and wish it was bigger, but basically I'm happy." A piece of chocolate broke off his ice cream and tumbled to the grass. He eyed it, weighing whether to pick it up and eat it or let it rest, and opted for the latter. "Besides," he added, "I like the people in government, and investment banking is populated by bastards. How about you—do you miss dancing?"

"All the time. I still remember the first

performance I saw at Lincoln Center after I'd left the company. I just sat there in the audience crying like an idiot, because I realized I'd never dance again. I guess that was the end of innocence, my fantasy existence, if you will. After that, I had to go out and face the real world." They finished their ice cream, and stood up to walk. "I'll get by," Hannah added, finishing that part of the conversation. "We both will. But the truth is, neither of us really has what we want."

"What do you mean?"

"Come off it, Fergy. We know each other too well for that. You go out with an endless stream of women you don't really want to be with. I sit home because I haven't found whatever it is I'm looking for. Neither of us is satisfied."

The strength of her emotions caught him by surprise.

"Look at us," Hannah continued. "Look at you. When was the last time you felt you were in love? How many times have you told me that you know how to have a relationship, but you're not doing it because you haven't found a woman you want to share your life with?"

"I'm not sure what you're saying."

"What I'm saying is, we're on a carousel, both of us. All I hear from you is your relationship with Miss X is doomed because she snores. You went out with Miss Y and her breasts are so big that, instead of *Playboy*, she belongs in *National Geographic*. Madame Z isn't very bright and she bit you. Right now, what I see in both of us, and particularly you, is that we know what our feelings and desires should be, not what they are."

"You're not pulling any punches today, are you."

"But I'm right, aren't I?"

There was no answer.

"Aren't I?" she demanded.

"Maybe."

Why was she pushing like this? Hannah wondered. What had spurred her tirade? Usually they joked about Fergy's dates. "I don't know," she said out loud. "I suppose neither of us is the best-analyzed person in the world. Probably we rank midway between a healthy person and Kyle."

That was it: Kyle! Working his way back into her thoughts again. Kyle was the cause.

"If he calls," Fergy offered, "tell him to come over and look at the bumps and calluses on your dancer's feet. That should get rid of him."

Hannah didn't want humor; not now, anyway. And she didn't want to get sucked into Kyle's problems, but here she was, in the park on a sunny afternoon, reacting to Kyle.

The situation was unsettling—unsettling and strange. Sometimes in bed at night she would ask herself, "Who is it I dream about?

What does he look like? Does he have a name?" But for Kyle, the fantasy was infinitely simpler: it was Hannah.

"I don't want to be on a pedestal," she said aloud, looking toward Fergy. "Not for Kyle—not for anyone. It makes me airsick."

Fergy smiled.

But flippant remarks couldn't change what was happening, couldn't obscure the fact that Hannah was growing more and more worried. With increasing frequency she was thinking about Kyle. There was something about him—certain emotions he hadn't exhibited but which she knew were there. How could she explain it? Maybe by analogy to black holes. Astronomers couldn't see the holes directly, but because of what happened around them, they knew they were there.

Enough, Hannah told herself. Kyle was jumbling her thoughts. It frightened her to speculate on what it was that had impelled him to insert himself into her life now.

□ □ □

Richard Marritt sat at his desk, eating a chocolate chip cookie, talking with his partner, Jim Dema. Marritt didn't like holidays. The Fourth of July and New Year's Eve were prime time for fireworks, and it was astounding how many of the explosions echoing through the city were revelers' gunshots. Halloween?

"There's a million people running around in masks," he'd once complained, "and I always think half of them are muggers." Christmas? "You got all those people robbing other people, and then the judge lets them off because they say they needed money to buy presents for their loved ones." Thanksgiving? "Thanksgiving I like. In fact, once I helped carry the Snoopy balloon in Macy's Thanksgiving Day Parade."

Biting into the cookie, Marritt wondered which designer brand—David's, Mrs. Fields, Famous Amos—it was. In the old days the best cookies in New York had been made by Schrafft's. That was when Schrafft's fudge sauce was something outstanding, and its bakery goods equal to the best. But it was pointless to reminisce about that era with Dema because, like President Kennedy, Schrafft's had been before the younger cop's time.

"My wife says we're rearranging the living room furniture this weekend," the detective offered. "A new look, she calls it. Actually, I think she just wants me to move the sofa so she can vacuum behind it."

"Tell her you can't because of your back."

"I did. All that happened was she gave me a dirty look and I felt guilty." Finishing his cookie, Marritt reached for the *Daily News*, which was on his desk, sports section up. "The Mets lost again," he said, shaking his head. "The Yankees too.... And the mayor was at the game," he reported, reading further. "That must have been a real thrill for everyone in attendance." Flipping the paper over, the detective scanned the "happy holiday" headline, then turned to page two and resumed a running commentary. "Sturbridge Jewelers was indicted yesterday for helping customers evade state and city sales tax. A lot of these stores, they're really something. You wouldn't believe how much of their business is jewelry for mistresses. Clients go in, look at rings and bracelets in special back rooms; they even have secret entrances and exits."

Next page.

"I see the governor is at it again. More money for unemployment, less money for cops. If you want my opinion, what they ought to do is make everyone on unemployment work for it—some sort of public service work like reading to old people or sweeping the streets. If they did that, you'd be amazed how many people on unemployment would find jobs in a hurry."

Page four—stories on tax reform and a shooting incident in South Africa.

Page five—"Oh, shit! Look at this."

Leaning forward, Dema saw the headline in solid block letters: EAST SIDE REDHEAD SLAIN IN APARTMENT. Then Marritt was reading aloud, looking up from the newspaper periodically to make eye contact with his partner.

" 'A thirty-two-year-old Manhattan social

worker was found stabbed to death yesterday evening in her apartment at Sixty East Twenty-ninth Street. Police say that the body of Alison Schoenfeld was discovered by a neighbor, who came to visit, heard music coming from inside the apartment, and found the door unlocked. Thirteenth Precinct officials report that Miss Schoenfeld's fully clothed body was on the living room floor. Her carotid artery had been slashed by a simple thrust, and she appeared to have died at approximately seven o'clock last night.' "

Marritt felt a sinking sensation in the pit of his stomach.

" 'Friends and relatives were shocked by Miss Schoenfeld's death. "She was the last person this sort of thing should happen to," said Marie Trucott, who lived—' "

Skipping the accolades, the detective searched for further substantive information: " 'There was no evidence of sexual molestation. . . . No sign of forced entry or theft. . . . Miss Schoenfeld was the second young woman stabbed to death in her apartment in recent weeks. Sixteen days ago, Linda Taylor of Two-fifty-nine West Seventy-sixth Street—'

"Not the second—the third," Marritt muttered. "Now I remember. There was another one on the East Side—Ethel something, back in April."

"Are you sure?" Dema asked.

"Of course I'm sure. I read about it in the

newspaper. That's three murders in three different precincts, with the same essentials in each."

"Maybe it's coincidence."

"I don't believe in coincidences; not like this." Laying the newspaper aside, Marritt began to think aloud, juggling the basics of each case. "Linda Taylor was stabbed to death. Her carotid artery was slashed. There was no sign of forced entry or sexual molestation, and her body was fully clothed on the floor of her apartment. Sixteen days later, the same thing happened to Alison Schoenfeld. And I'll lay odds that Ethel what's-her-name was in the same condition when they found her, but with all the police precincts in this city, you have to read about it in the newspaper before the pieces fit."

Dema waited, confident that his mentor would continue as he usually did. This time, though, there was silence. "What are you thinking?" he asked at last.

There was more silence, accompanied by a weary look on Marritt's face. Then, finally—

"I was thinking," the detective said slowly, "that lack of communication between police precincts isn't the problem. The real problem is that somewhere in this city there's a lunatic who's very good at murdering people. And I doubt very much that whatever started him on this rampage has been resolved."

Chapter 9

THE REST OF THE HOLIDAY WEEKEND WENT ABOUT as expected for Hannah. She read, watched television, went shopping, and had dinner with a date who grew decidedly more boring as the evening wore on. After they'd said good night and he indicated that he'd had a wonderful time and would call again, Hannah asked herself why she went out at all. Like Fergy, she never seemed to find the relationship she thought she was looking for. Unlike Fergy, she disliked the pursuit and had no interest in fleeting sexual liaisons.

The third headless rose came on Monday—in a long narrow box wrapped in brown paper, postmarked the fifth of July. Even before Hannah opened the package, she knew what was inside: dead leaves, a stem, and a plain white card with the letters *THHIRWRDNK*. She stared at the card and headless rose for a long time. Why? That was all she could think to ask. Why?

Also in the mail was a bill from MasterCard

95

and a plain white envelope with a West 88th Street return address. Hannah opened the envelope and found a teddy bear greeting card with a handwritten message inside:

> O my love, my darling
> I've hungered for your touch
> A long lonely time
>
> > Love,
> > Kyle

"Unchained Melody"; one good song ruined forever. From now on, whenever she heard it she would think of Kyle.

The handwriting on the card didn't match the handwriting on the brown paper wrapper that came with the roses. The greeting card and envelope were in script, most likely Kyle's normal handwriting. The brown wrapper was marked with squat printed letters that appeared fashioned with the aid of a ruler.

> Time goes by so slowly, and time can do so much
> Are you still mine?

Against Hannah's will, the song lyrics reverberated through her mind:

> I need your love
> God speed your love
> To me

Hannah crumpled the envelope and card, stuffed them in the rose box, and threw the package out. Then she took the subway to class, burying herself in teaching to drive away visions of Kyle.

"Daniele, you're still not holding the third position long enough. . . . Sherry, keep your knees together or it doesn't count. . . . Joanna, lower your right hand."

The next day began with laundry and straightening up the apartment, then pizza for lunch. One of the few things Hannah liked about not being a professional dancer anymore was the freedom to eat what she wanted. She took a walk, wrote some letters, and taught two more hours of class. Afterward, there was her ritual bath, followed by dinner alone while reading *The New York Times*. The front page of the newspaper was typically somber. In the lower lefthand corner of the page, the headline POLICE LINK MIDTOWN MURDERS caught her eye. Munching on an avocado and cheese sandwich, she began to read:

New York City Police Department officials announced today that they believe the same killer is responsible for the stabbing murders of three Manhattan women this year. Each victim was found in her apartment,

97

fully clothed, with no sign of forced entry or theft. Addressing a group of reporters at One Police Plaza, Lieutenant Richard Marritt confirmed that matching fingerprints had been found in the apartments of Ethel Purcell, Linda Taylor and Alison Schoenfeld. Miss Purcell was stabbed to death on April 18th; Miss Taylor on June 17th; Miss Schoenfeld on July 3d.

Marritt stated that a reconstruction of events indicates each of the women was in midtown Manhattan shortly before her death. Police speculate that, in each instance, the killer may have befriended his victim in a public place and been invited to her home. "As of now," the detective explained, "we have fingerprints but no suspect who matches them. We'd welcome any help the public can provide."

Normally, Hannah didn't read crime stories, but this time identification with the victims led her on:

"I don't know how to say this," Marritt told reporters, "except to say, every time a woman lets a man she doesn't know into her apartment, she's putting herself in danger."

98

Appearing at the same press conference, New York City Chief of Detectives Harvey Granfort announced that the police investigation of the killings had been placed under a unified command. "Capturing this lunatic is a high departmental priority," declared Granfort.

A special 30-man task force has been set up under the guidance of Lieutenant Marritt, who last year won praise for his investigation of the murders of three musicians at New York's Lincoln Center. Members of the public with information that might aid in solving these latest crimes should call—

The ring of Hannah's own telephone interrupted. Putting the receiver to her ear, she greeted the caller.

"Hello?"

"Hi, this is Kyle."

If there was anyone in the world she didn't want to hear from at the moment, it was Kyle. He was number one on the list—possibly number two, behind Muammar Qaddafy.

"I just called to see how you've been lately."

"I'm okay," Hannah answered.

"What have you been doing?"

"Nothing special."

99

"I guess things have been pretty quiet for me, too. I was wondering, would you like to get together for lunch tomorrow?"

"I can't. I'm busy."

"How abut Thursday?"

"I'm busy then, too."

"Friday, or maybe sometime this weekend?"

"Look, Kyle, I'm trying to be nice to you, but I just don't think it's good for us to go out together."

"Well, sure—I mean, I understand you don't want us to really date, but I don't see the harm in getting together as friends."

Hannah felt herself growing exasperated. "Kyle, we're not friends. I don't want to have lunch with you; I don't want to take walks with you. I think it's time you faced up to reality."

"But you don't know me. If you took the time, you'd understand. I'm worthy of you, really I am."

This is lunacy, Hannah told herself. He's off-the-wall bonkers.

"I know you don't feel about me the way I feel about you. I accept that. But—"

"Kyle, I'm going to hang up."

"Just listen—for one minute—please. I remember everything about the first time I saw you. I was nervous because it was the first day of school; I'd transferred and had no friends. I'd hated my old school, but at least I'd known people. Then my family moved, and I had to start all over again in eleventh grade."

She really should hang up.

"It was the first day of school. I'd had four classes, and no one had said a word to me. I hadn't talked to anyone. And then I saw you. It was in Mr. Quinn's English class. You were wearing a blue skirt and a white sweater. I'd never seen anyone like you. And you said hello. You were the first person in the school I even talked to."

"Kyle, this is now. We're thirty-five years old."

"Don't you understand? I go to bed at night pretending I'm with you. I wake up at five in the morning thinking about you. I've never been with another woman when I didn't want to be with you. There's—"

"Stop it!"

"I can't stop. Please, just listen to me. If only we could be friends, I'd never take you for granted. I'd always be there for you."

He's flipping out, Hannah decided. He's going off the deep end.

"Do you know what it's like for me to spend my life with a sinking feeling every time I think about you? Do you know what it's like waiting by the phone hoping you'll call?"

"Don't wait. I'm not calling."

"But you have to!"

"Kyle, leave me alone. Chase some other fantasy."

"But I have no fantasy except you."

The tone of desperation in his voice verged on the ominous.

"Look, Kyle, this isn't good; you're scaring me. I don't want you to call again. I don't want you to send any more cards. Please, just leave me alone."

Then there was silence.

"Hannah, I love you."

"I'm hanging up now."

"Please don't. Just—"

Click.

□   □   □

Fergy was playing records on the stereo in his bedroom when Hannah called. For several minutes, he listened as she recounted Kyle's latest outpouring of emotion.

"I've got to hand it to you," he said when her tale of woe was done. "When it comes to men, you sure know how to pick 'em."

"I didn't pick him. He wrote me a letter and then he called for dinner."

"But you went out with him, and then you saw him again for a walk after you knew he was a nut."

"Don't yell at me, Fergy. I need help."

"Hold on. I have to turn the stereo off."

There was a pause, during which Crosby,

Stills and Nash faded into oblivion. Then Fergy came back on the line again. "I've got a question for you: what's Hannah spelled backward?"

She wasn't in the mood.

"All right," he said. "Let's put our heads together and see what we come up with. Why is Kyle Howard obsessed with you?"

"How should I know?"

"You're not thinking, Banana. Try to get into the spirit of things. Obviously he's had a crush on you since high school. And just as obviously, you're only a catalyst for problems he had long before he met you."

"So?"

"So this is a guy who, by definition, was thoroughly miserable by the time he reached puberty. Then he saw you. You were beautiful; you were nice to him; and given your home life, you were miserable too. Plus you were a ballerina, symbolic of beauty, grace, perfection and strength—the perfect fantasy."

"But that was eighteen years ago. Fergy, you don't seem to understand. When Kyle said two weeks ago that he's been obsessed with me for years, he was being literal. I'm not exaggerating. He's been obsessed with me for almost twenty years."

There was a pause as Fergy evaluated what to say next. Maybe Kyle has a list of women he's obsessed with, he was tempted to offer. But under the circumstances, he didn't think Hannah would find the suggestion humorous.

103

"Let me ask you something," he said at last. "That night when Kyle told you he dreams about you—did he say what kind of dreams?"

"I didn't ask."

"Do you think they're violent?"

"No. And, Fergy, I don't want to know."

She also wished Fergy hadn't asked that particular question, since she was frightened enough without it.

"I've got an idea," he told her. "Send him a turd."

"What?"

"Send him a turd. Hannah, it's perfect. Wrap it in tin foil, put it in a box, wrap the box in brown paper, and send it through the mail with a card that reads 'THHIR' or whatever the letters he sends you are. There's no law against sending shit through the mail."

"Fergy, you're sick."

"I know, but it's a great idea. What better way to get even for his sending you dead roses?"

"That's beside the point. I don't want to get even. I want to get rid of him."

"Maybe he won't call again."

"And maybe he will."

"Why don't you get an unlisted number?"

"Because I don't want to cut myself off from the rest of the world."

There was a silence.

"What are you thinking?" Hannah prodded.

"Not much. I'm just trying to figure out

what's going on in Kyle's mind. He's thirty-five, maybe thirty-six years old. Probably, his fantasies aren't enough to sustain and protect him against reality anymore. You're the focus of everything he thinks is desirable, so he's decided to contact you. He needs help, but unless it comes from you, he doesn't want it. I don't know; I suppose there's a little of Kyle in all of us."

"Is that supposed to make me feel sorry for him?"

"Not at all. There's no mercy intended. It's just that too many fantasies can screw up your life. I know. I still spend time thinking about women from long ago, ghosts from the past and fantasies of the future."

"Who are you, Fergy? You say things like that, and sometimes I'm not sure I know."

"Neither am I. But looking back, I'm inclined to think I should have gotten married ten years ago. That way, it would be out of my system, I could stop worrying about women, and I'd be happily divorced by now."

"Sweetheart, I've got news for you. Going through a divorce isn't easy. Although in my case it was enjoyable compared with the marriage."

Fergy laughed. "Actually, I can understand Kyle. I've got a pretty good crush on you myself."

"That's different, Fergy. We're friends."

They talked for an hour.

"Consider yourself hugged," were the last words Hannah spoke to him before they said good night.

Then Fergy went to bed, wishing he was good enough for Hannah, but knowing he wasn't; telling himself that Kyle wasn't the only one who drifted from time to time into fantasies of spending a lifetime with her.

Chapter 10

COPS SELDOM GET REGULARLY SCHEDULED DAYS off. Instead, it's Monday and Tuesday one month, something else the next. For July, Wednesday and Thursday were Marritt's days of rest.

Wednesday the ninth, he took David and Jonathan to the beach. Coming home they stopped at McDonald's, where Jonathan ordered a "hamburger au gratin." ("Grade school French," Marritt explained to the counter clerk.) Thursday, the detective helped David organize his collection of bottle caps. Then he cleaned the apartment and cooked dinner to give his wife a break. Getting back to the 20th Precinct would be a vacation, except there were three murders to contend with.

Friday morning, Marritt rode the subway into Manhattan, transferred to the B train at Rockefeller Center, and arrived at the stationhouse at eight o'clock. Dema was waiting, and they conferred in the detective's second-floor office.

Because of the murders, the room had been transformed. On one wall, there was a large street map of Manhattan with red dots signifying the murder sites. Thin colored lines traced the movements of each victim on the day of her death: blue for Ethel Purcell, green for Linda Taylor, brown for Alison Schoenfeld. A stack of folders lay on the detective's desk. Every interview with friends, neighbors, co-workers, and relatives had been written up. Names and addresses culled from datebooks had been cross-indexed. For each crime, the detective had noted the victim's age, background, appearance, the type of building she lived in, even the weather. Every last scrap of evidence had been processed with one concrete result: the fingerprints matched.

A three-by-six-inch fingerprint card lay face up on Marritt's desk. The killer was good at what he did. Each victim lived in a building without a doorman or elevator operator. No one had reported seeing any of the women just prior to their deaths. Most likely, the perpetrator met his victims in public, accompanied them home, and if anyone saw them together, let them live. But he left fingerprints—on drinking glasses, doorknobs, faucets—fingerprints that were now in the hands of police technicians engaged in the laborious, time-consuming task of reviewing the prints of every known sex offender and knife assailant in the City of New York. And when that task was complete, the range of suspects would be broadened to include all those released from mental hospitals and perpetrators of violent assaults.

"I've never been on a case like this," Marritt said, beginning the conversation with Dema. "Most murders have a certain logic. They're family quarrels, robberies, something like that. Here there's nothing concrete to go on."

"We've got fingerprints."

"Yeah, we've got fingerprints, but not much else. The perpetrator is probably between twenty-five and forty. You have to figure it that way because of the women's ages. And he's fairly strong; otherwise, he couldn't kill as efficiently as he does with a single thrust. But beyond that, it's guesswork. Probably he's white. Most likely he lives in the city, but maybe he comes in from the suburbs. He could be straight, gay, an accountant, even a cop."

Dema waited as Marritt continued his thoughts.

"There's thousands of deranged people walking the streets: bag ladies, old men shouting obscenities and masturbating in public, people who haven't bathed for six months. This guy isn't even one of them. If he was, three women wouldn't have let him into their apartments."

The telephone rang, and Marritt picked up the receiver. "That's right," Dema heard him grumble. "Take his name, but don't book him for murder. . . . Because the prints don't match. . . . No, the same prints were found in each apartment. That means one guy committed all three murders, and we're not going to help every nut who comes in to confess to get his picture in the newspaper."

"That was number three," the detective said after he'd hung up.

"Number three?"

"Yeah. The third psycho who's come in to confess. It happens all the time when a murder's written up in the newspapers, especially the *Post*. All you can do is take their name, refer them for psychiatric study, and hope they don't decide to really kill someone. But to change the subject, what's happening with the lab reports?"

"Nothing new. Like you said, the fingerprints match. The hairs are a probable match, but inconclusive."

"And the FBI material on serial killers?"

"It's on your desk."

Looking down, Marritt rummaged through a pile of papers until he came to a forty-page report with the FBI logo imprinted on top. "All right. Why don't you start on yesterday's interview sheets. It's amazing how much paper work thirty detectives generate. I'll see what I can get out of this report."

Dema left. Marritt took off his jacket, decided against getting a cup of coffee, and settled behind his desk with the FBI data.

"There are 5,000 unsolved homicides in the United States each year," began the report:

> Over half are believed to be the work of serial killers. Unlike mass murderers, who crack suddenly and kill a group of people in one incident, serial murderers kill repeatedly, often for years on end. Most serial murderers wet their bed in childhood, played with fire, and tortured animals. The average serial murderer is an unmarried man between the ages of 30 and 40. Eighty percent are white. Eight percent are women. About ten percent are doctors, dentists or other health care professionals. Serial murderers are above average in intelligence, and seem quite normal, even charming, on a daily basis. Most experts believe that they cannot be reformed. They are untreatable, unrehabilitable, and uncontrollable. The serial killer rarely knows his victim. He kills without remorse, and is impelled by a blood lust that is seldom satiated.

Next came thumbnail biographies of a dozen serial killers:

EDMUND KEMPER: 6'9" tall, 280 pounds, IQ rated at borderline-genius. At age 16 Kemper killed his grandmother. Considered a model inmate at the mental institution where he spent five years after the murder, he was paroled at age 21. Thereafter, he murdered six young women in the San Francisco Bay area. Often, after having sex with the victim's corpse, he severed the limbs and carried the torso to his bedroom for further orgies. Kemper finally surrendered to police after bludgeoning his mother to death, cutting off her head, propping it on a hatbox, and using it as a dartboard. Sentenced to life imprisonment in 1973, he is now eligible for parole.

"Great," Marritt muttered to himself. "Let's see who's next."

JOHN GACY: A Chicago building contractor who earned $200,000 a year, was a member of the Jaycees, and murdered 33 boys and young men. Gacy invited victims to his home for job interviews on nights when his wife was out, strangled them to death, and buried them under his house.

Often he would recite the 23rd Psalm while murdering his victims. When captured, Gacy made a point of telling reporters that he was bisexual, not a homosexual, because he didn't want the public-at-large to look down on him.

HENRY LEE LUCAS: Lucas has confessed to murdering 360 men, women and children over a 24-year period. Approximately half of these killings have been verified by authorities. At age 23 he stabbed and strangled his mother before sexually penetrating her corpse. After six years in an institution for the criminally insane and eight more in prison, he was released from custody and began drifting around the country. Lucas boasts that he "crucified some victims and filleted others like fish." Recently he told an interviewer, "There isn't any way I haven't killed them. Killing someone is like walking outdoors. If I wanted a victim, I'd just go get one. Once I done a crime, I forget it."

Marritt was having trouble finding a frame of reference for the material he was readin victims Lucas was talking about v human beings like the detective's own wife and children.

THEODORE BUNDY: The glamour boy of serial murders; linked to the slaying of 40 young women. Bundy was a law school student in Utah, a onetime aide to Washington governor Dan Evans, and an architect of the Seattle Crime Prevention Commission's program to prevent rape. Hypnotically handsome and disarmingly charming, he frequently smashed his victim's skull before dumping the remains in an isolated mountain area.

The list went on:

Albert DeSalvo, the "Boston Strangler," murdered thirteen women between the ages of nineteen and eighty-five.

David Berkowitz, "Son of Sam"; also known as "the .44-caliber killer."

Juan Corona hacked to death twenty-five itinerant farm workers and buried them in shallow graves.

Patrick Kearney, an electronics engineer, admitted killing thirty-two boys and stuffing their dismembered remains in plastic bags.

Kenneth Bianchi, the "Hillside Strangler"; ─n murders. Bianchi was married, worked as ─ecurity guard, and was regarded by hometown police officials as "a good prospect for law enforcement work."

Wayne Williams, a music promoter and talent scout, convicted of killing two black youths in a series of twenty-eight Atlanta child murders.

Marritt couldn't read any more; he needed a break. Sometimes when he rode through areas of the city that were falling apart, he'd gaze at the buildings and wonder what they'd once looked like. Harlem, South Jamaica, the South Bronx—they hadn't been designed to turn to rubble. Once, they had been fresh and clean and full of promise. Probably, people who committed murder had been like that too, but it was hard to imagine them that way with crimes this monstrous.

He hoped the murders he was investigating would end with three dead. He was sure they wouldn't.

□ □ □

The package was delivered by parcel post. Hannah thought it looked like a box of typing paper, which it was—except this particular paper had already been typed on.

"The night we had dinner," read the accompanying note, "you said you wanted to see this. I'm delighted to share it with you. Love, Kyle."

Inside was Kyle's novel, untitled, 504 pages long.

115

Hannah stared at the manuscript. Then, impelled by a force she didn't fully understand, she began to read. It took twelve hours. She finished the book at four A.M.

There were two problems with the manuscript, Hannah decided when she was done. And she was trying hard to be objective as a means of warding off the terror that threatened to drag her down. The first problem was style. Each sentence was carefully crafted, too much so for the book's own good. Kyle couldn't write a line without incorporating at least one big word or carefully turned phrase. That might work for a nine- or ten-page short story, but for a lengthy novel, it was ponderous. The book fell of its own weight.

That was problem number one.

Problem number two was the plot. The book was clearly autobiographical. A young man grows up in Ohio, attends college at Amherst (Kyle had gone to Williams), then journeys to New York. He moves into an apartment in the West Eighties, buys a typewriter, and sets out to become an author. He struggles, meets and falls in love with a young woman (also a struggling author) who lives in the same building. In all respects, the hero is the heroine's pillar of strength. Then the woman dumps him in favor of a rich stockbroker, causing the hero to grieve for two hundred pages. In the end, of course, she comes back. Hero and heroine marry. He sells his first novel to a major publisher for a huge advance. She sells her first novel to an equally prestigious publisher for a smaller but nonetheless respectable advance. They will live happily ever after.

Very corny; also indisputedly frightening because the woman was Hannah.

The clothes the heroine wore were clothes Hannah had worn throughout her life. The stockbroker was patterned after Hannah's husband. The heroine did things Hannah had done, not just in high school but ever since.

It was now very clear that Kyle had been watching her for eighteen years.

PART THREE

Chapter 11

HANNAH WASN'T ALTOGETHER LUCID WHEN SHE telephoned Fergy on Saturday morning. Not that she should have been. After all, she'd been up reading until four o'clock, and then waited four hours more before calling for help. That meant she'd been awake for twenty-four hours when she dialed his number. And even well rested, it would have been hard to explain the 504 pages she'd just read considering the fact that she was scared stiff.

Fergy came over to her apartment, told Hannah to get some sleep, and took Kyle's novel home with him. Sunday morning he brought it back.

"I want you to know something, Banana. I broke a very important date to read this manuscript last night."

"And?"

"William Styron is better."

Midmorning sunlight filtered across the room. Hannah drank coffee, and Fergy sipped orange juice as they talked.

"It's me; I'm the love object in Kyle's novel. You know that, don't you?"

"It didn't take long to figure that out."

Reaching for the manuscript, Hannah brushed aside a strand of hair. "Listen—this is the part where Kyle is describing the stockbroker that the heroine, Helen, runs off with: 'David Hadley was born with a silver spoon—' "

"I know," Fergy interrupted. "You've told me about your husband, and I just spent twelve hours reading the book. You're Helen; Kyle is Ken. The entire book is his fantasy about loving you. In the sex scenes, he's fantasizing about being in bed with you. In the scenes where he grieves, he's grieving for you. When Ken goes to sleep at night hugging a pillow and pretending it's Helen, that's Kyle and you."

"But what's going on inside his head?"

"He's desperate; he's lonely. He's constructed a fantasy world to make up for the one he doesn't have, and now he's trapped inside it. He probably wants to go back and redo the past, but that's impossible, so the next best thing is pretending it never happened. That's why he's taken eighteen years and stuffed them in a novel, which leaves him free to pursue you like it was twelfth grade all over again."

"But there was never anything between us. You're talking as though Kyle and I had a relationship to fall back on. I hardly knew him."

"In his mind, you were lovers."

Hannah began turning manuscript pages again. "Listen. Ken keeps Helen's toothbrush in the bathroom after she's left, hoping she'll come back to him. In bed at night, he never sleeps for more than two hours without waking from a turbulent dream. The only way he can rise above his depression is by fantasizing her return."

"That's Kyle and you."

"And here—this is the part where she comes back to him:

"Helen: 'I've spent the past month living alone. I love you. I'm home to stay if you can find it in your heart to forgive me.'

"Ken: 'I love you, Helen.'

"Helen: 'You knew I'd come back, didn't you?'

"Ken: 'No. That's what made it all the more unbearable. That and the thought of someone else being with you.'

"And then they go to bed together," Hannah continued. "He's got his arms around her; they're both crying. I think I'll vomit."

"Try hard not to."

"Fergy—how do I get rid of him?"

"Maybe you could convince him to go into analysis. Suggest that, even though he's perfectly normal, if he went to a psychiatrist, he'd get marvelous material for another novel."

"Try again."

"All right—show him the creases on your rear end so he knows you're not perfect."

"Number one, I don't have creases on my rear end. Number two, go to hell. Fergy, this is serious."

"Okay, I apologize. But what else can you do? He's not breaking any law. He hasn't overtly threatened you. All he's done, really, is admit that he's hopelessly, obsessively, overwhelmingly in love. Look, sending this novel might have been his last hurrah. Send it back; don't talk to him. With luck, he'll be gone."

"And without luck?"

"You can deal with that contingency if and when it happens."

When it happens, Hannah told herself, because she didn't feel particularly lucky at the moment. But at least she had Fergy to see her through.

"I owe you," she told him.

"That's what friends are for. But in case you'd like to buy me a present, a trip to Paris would be lovely."

"I was thinking of something in the five-dollar range, maybe ten. Come on, I'll treat you to brunch."

"I'd love it, but that very important date I broke last night has been rescheduled for this afternoon. And if I break it again, the next time you see me I might be turning over a fire on a spit with an apple in my mouth."

□ □ □

Sunday afternoon.

There were three stages—the search for a victim, the seduction, and the act itself. The search was easy. So many women were there to be taken, and the only prerequisite was that the victim seem right. This one with the red hair. She's fine.

The seduction was harder, more challenging and complex. But sometimes it wasn't hard at all.

"What are you looking at?"

"You."

"Well?"

"I'm impressed."

That wasn't so difficult. Often he was rebuffed, but inevitably someone would respond.

Elizabeth . . . That's a nice name. . . . Talk to her gently. Be charming. . . . I like Sundays too. What time is it? Five o'clock. Relax. Spend some time with her. An hour. More. No doorman. No elevator operator. It's a nice apartment, but the chair is uncomfortable, too deep; the kind of chair I like to sink into, but I want to sit up straight now.

She's teasing.

"Do you always sit like a schoolboy? So straight and tall?"

125

The last one had red hair too. Take her. It's la-la time. She doesn't understand.

"Why?"

"It's a game."

Her breasts are growing. You fuck the body and make love to the soul. All time is unfolding. Texture. Colors. Wet red. Breasts like cannonballs. This one is good. She knows how to lie still when it's over.

Wash my hands. Go home. I'll send a rose to Hannah tomorrow.

Chapter 12

MONADY STARTED SLOWLY FOR MARRITT. HE got up, ate breakfast, shaved, showered, and put on a suit. Usually the process took an hour; this time it consumed ninety minutes. Just before leaving for work, he looked in the mirror, decided he didn't like the tie he was wearing, and changed to another. The subway broke down between Woodhaven Boulevard and Grand Avenue. The changeover at Rockefeller Center seemed endless. By the time the detective arrived at the 20th Precinct stationhouse, it was ten o'clock. Together with Dema, he reviewed interview sheets compiled over the weekend. Nothing. Then he turned to fingerprint reports. In about a year, the department was expected to install a computer system for matching prints. When that happened, the killer's legacy could be compared virtually instantaneously with one million prints on file at police headquarters, but until then, comparisons would have to made manually. Marritt didn't have until next year.

Not that it mattered. Something about the killer made people trust him. Well-educated women invited him into their homes. Marritt didn't think his name would be on file at police headquarters—not yet, anyway.

Another report on serial killers came in from the FBI. For the rest of the morning the detective studied its contents:

> Serial murderers and the single-outburst mass murderer are two separate types. The mass murderer, beleaguered by pressure, explodes at a single moment, exhausts himself in a violent frenzy, and is unlikely to kill again. By contrast, serial killers are sexual sadists. They derive pleasure from killing their victims, and repeat again and again until captured. A high percentage of serial murderers are born to unwed mothers and prostitutes. During their first three years of life, the bonding process is somehow flawed; mother and child develop a sadistic aggressive relationship toward one another. Unable and afraid to express anger against the mother, the child decides to appease his tormentor, but a deep-seated rage has begun to burn. Revenge will come later.

Marritt read on. As with the earlier FBI material, there were thumbnail sketches of various serial killers:

Richard Chase, the "Vampire Killer" of California, who ate pieces of his victims' bodies.

Joseph Kallinger, the Philadelphia shoemaker who murdered three people in a continuing orgy with his own son.

"Enough," said Marritt. Then he realized he was talking out loud. Not a good sign. It was twelve o'clock, time for lunch. But after what he'd just read, the detective didn't feel like eating. His wife's birthday was coming up. Maybe he should go out and buy her a present, except he had no idea what she wanted.

Dema returned and talked Marritt into going out for something to eat. They chose a coffee shop two blocks from the precinct house. "Murders are crazy," the detective posited between mouthfuls of hamburger. "They're always different from what they seem."

"What do you mean?"

"I'll give you an example. Ten years ago I had a case where this guy went to bed with his girlfriend. Then he went home without spending the night. A burglar broke in, and the woman was killed. From the lab tests, we thought she'd been raped. Another time, I had a case where a white guy came home and found his wife naked on the floor under-

129

neath a black man with a lot of screaming and groaning going on, so he grabbed a kitchen knife and killed the black guy, figuring him for a rapist. Then it turned out it wasn't rape. The black guy was his wife's lover."

"What happened to the husband?"

"A jury let him off. Probably, it would have been different if the colors were reversed, but that's the way it is. Someday you're gonna have a white man in a three-piece business suit who goes around robbing black teenagers at knife-point, and nobody will believe the teen-agers."

After lunch they went back to the precinct house. Dema began sifting through papers. Marritt called home to see what his wife wanted for a birthday present.

"Shit," the younger cop heard his mentor grumble. "All right, all right. It's your birth-day. I'll do it."

"What is it?" Dema asked when the conver-sation was over.

"You won't believe what my wife wants."

"I'm listening."

"You can listen all you want. It won't make life easier. My wife says it's time we added spice to our marriage; something about how we only have sex when there's nothing good on television. I'm supposed to go out and buy her a sexy bra. . . . Don't look at me like that. One word and I'll take your head off."

□ □ □

She looked so pretty in the yearbook graduation portrait, wearing a white sweater and single strand of pearls. God, he loved that photograph. The Latin Honor Society entry wasn't as flattering, but it showed them together. He'd been close enough that morning to reach out and touch her, caress her hair. The Drama Workshop photo was the most enticing—Hannah, full-length, dressed in a leotard with her hair down. Still, the graduation portrait was more moving. It captured her spirit, her smile, and eyes.

Dust balls lay on the floor of Kyle's apartment. The bed was unmade. He remembered seeing Hannah in a white bathing suit at Lake Hume in August, eighteen years before. He'd seen her cleavage, the outline of her nipples against white nylon, beads of water on her body glistening in the sun. He'd looked away then, and turned back when he hoped Hannah wasn't looking. She'd sparkled, like an angel. Probably, she didn't have the bathing suit anymore; eighteen years was a long time. If only he could go back, knowing what he knew now.

Is she reading my novel? I'm lonely without her. Rejection, dejection, erection, ejection. I remember the first time she talked to me in school—what she said, even what she wore. And the assembly that night in winter when she performed on stage, the glimmer of the moon against frost on the window panes.

Maybe I should call to make sure she has the novel. Once she's read it, she'll call. Should I wait or call first, or write? Probably I should give her time to read the novel. Tuesday. Wednesday at the latest. Then, if she hasn't called, I'll call.

Hannah, I love you. And I had a dream. I was back in high school, and I was naked and alone. And in the dream, everyone came running from the classrooms to look and stare, and all I cared about was that you didn't see me. Because I was afraid if you saw me, like the others, you'd be cruel. I could endure anything in the world but that from you. The moment I saw you, I knew what my life was for. . . .

□ □ □

Five o'clock. Bloomingdale's. Never again, Marritt muttered to himself as he walked through the entrance at Lexington Avenue and 59th Street. There are plainclothes cops all over this joint because Ethel Purcell had a sales slip that showed she was here the day she got murdered, and every one of them will be looking at me. I have every right to be embarrassed. . . . Where the hell is the lingerie department? I feel like a pervert. If I get stopped by a cop for looking at bras, I can always say I came to do a little detective work. This is worse than the first time I bought a condom. . . . Here it is: lingerie. Three saleswomen. The oldest looks the safest. Yes, ma'am; I'd like to buy a bra. . . . No, it's not for myself. You're just what I need—a female Milton Berle. . . . Size 36B, I think. . . . I don't know. What's the difference between a bra that opens in front and one that hooks in the back? . . . For my wife. She'd like it if it was sexy. . . . I can't help it if I look embarrassed. Just show me the bra.

Marritt got home at six o'clock.

"The commissioner called," his wife told him. "There's been another murder."

Chapter 13

THE FOLLOWING MORNING; ELEVEN O'CLOCK.

Marritt hated press conferences. Reporters only made life difficult, and the bigger the problem, the more reporters there were on hand. At the moment, the press room at One Police Plaza was jammed. Sitting beneath a bank of television lights, the detective listened and waited his turn.

"Good morning, ladies and gentlemen. I'm Harvey Granfort, Chief of Detectives of the New York City Police Department. As all of you know, yesterday afternoon at four o'clock, the body of a young woman named Elizabeth Wald was found in her apartment at One-twelve Hudson Street in Manhattan. Miss Wald was last seen by a friend two days ago, on Sunday morning. A preliminary autopsy indicates that she was killed Sunday evening at approximately seven o'clock. As with three previous victims, Miss Wald was stabbed to death by a single thrust to the carotid artery. Fingerprints found in her apartment match

135

those found in the apartments of Ethel Purcell, Linda Taylor, and Alison Schoenfeld. As of today, the number of detectives assigned to the case has been increased from thirty to fifty. The man in charge of the investigation is Lieutenant Richard Marritt, who is here to answer questions for you now."

Slowly, to the accompanying rustle of pages turning on note pads, Marritt stepped to the podium. "I don't have much to say," he began. "You all know that four women have been murdered. Each victim was stabbed to death. There's no evidence of sexual molestation or forced entry to any of the apartments. I know this case is generating an enormous amount of fear and concern. We appreciate the gravity of the situation and are doing the best we can. That's it. Are there any questions?"

Television cameras rolled. An array of hands shot into the air.

"Sir, could you give us any profile of the killer?"

"Based on microscopic hair examination, we believe he's a white male."

"What else?"

"That's all. Beyond that, everything is speculation."

"Are there any suspects?"

"No."

"Do you have a theory as to why the killer doesn't sexually molest his victims?"

How should I know, Marritt wanted to

answer. Maybe he's afraid of getting herpes. "At the present time, we just don't know the answer to that. Most likely, the gratification experienced by the killer lies in the exercise of life and death power over his victims."

"Is there any estimate regarding the killer's age?"

"Based on the age of the victims and histories of other serial murderers, we believe he's between twenty-five and forty, but I want to emphasize that's only speculation. We also assume he's relatively strong and agile based on the nature of the wounds inflicted."

"Could you elaborate on that?"

"Each of the victims was stabbed to death by a single knife thrust to the carotid artery. I'm told by our medical staff that it takes a very powerful direct thrust to cut through the muscle that protects the artery. Once could be luck. But to kill with a single thrust on four separate occasions indicates strength, quickness, and a certain knowledge of anatomy."

"Are you saying it's possible that the killer is a doctor?"

"Anything is possible."

The questions kept coming; the television lights got hotter.

"Is there a target group that the police are focusing on in this investigation?"

"So far, we've placed primary emphasis on people with a history of violent sexual crimes and assaults, but even that limited target group is difficult to cover. Thousands of sex offenders are released from New York prisons and psychiatric hospitals each year. All anyone has to do is walk the streets to realize there are thousands of people in need of treatment, and we simply don't have the manpower to bring them all in for questioning. And even if we did, based on the rapport we believe the killer had with his victims, he probably wouldn't be among them."

"Is there anything the public can do to help?"

"Obviously we don't want to be inundated with false leads, but somebody out there knows this guy. Most likely, he's not a person who draws attention to himself. He seems normal on a superficial level and looks like everyone else. But if members of the public have what they believe is a reasonable suspicion, they should report it. All calls will be kept in confidence."

"Do you have any idea what triggers the killings?"

"No."

"Do you think the killer actually wants to be caught?"

"Judging by what we've seen so far, he seems to be going to great lengths to insure the opposite."

"Would you say that your reputation within

138

the department as one of New York's best detectives is on the line with this case?"

"I couldn't care less. All my reputation means is that once or twice I got lucky."

"Do you think the killer will strike again?"

It was the panic question; and there was only one honest answer.

"This individual," Marritt said slowly, "has a compulsion to commit murder. We can't put a cop in every single woman's apartment. We're going on the assumption that, unless stopped, he'll kill again."

The press conference lasted just short of an hour. When it was over, Marritt stopped in the cafeteria for a doughnut and coffee, then took the elevator to a fourth-floor conference room for a noon meeting with the detectives assigned to the case. Fifty men were on hand, far and away the largest number Marritt had ever had working for him. About a dozen faces were familiar, the rest strangers.

"All right," Marritt told the cops gathered in front of him, "you know why we're here. You're professionals, and I won't repeat what you already know. I just want to emphasize that good police work is part art and part science. This case will be solved based on your ability to collect and evaluate evidence. Here's what we have to do."

For the next hour, the detective ran through a list of procedures to be followed in the investigation. Every lead would be given a follow-up rating—immediate, solid, if-and-when, or never. Because sex crimes are progressive, special attention would be paid to leads involving instances of indecent exposure, rape, and deviant behavior.

"For the time being, I want to minimize efforts to enlist the public," Marritt continued. "Obviously, people will be aware of the case, but too many appeals for public assistance will cause panic. Sometime within the next week we'll be given access to a computer that will enable us to cross-reference clues and miscellaneous data. From now on, anytime anyone is arrested in the City of New York, his fingerprints will be matched against prints found in the victims' apartments. I don't know how good this guy is. Maybe he has street smarts; maybe he's just lucky. But he'll be hard to catch, and any future murder will have an exponential effect in terms of panic. That's about it except for one thing more. No job is perfect, but if we catch this guy, we'll have made the world a better place to live."

The meeting broke up at two o'clock. Marritt went back to the cafeteria for a sandwich, then out to the street where a squad car was waiting to take him back to the precinct house. You wonder what this killer lives with day in and day out, the detective told himself. Four women dead in a three-month period. Life could be dangerous; the city was helpless.

Then Marritt saw the headline—flashed by a newspaperboy on the street—and it just about drove him crazy, because every instinct the detective possessed told him it would force the killer to strike again. In the upper lefthand corner of the *New York Post*, page one, there was a bold type lead-in: Fourth Manhattan Woman Slain. And beneath it, in a type size normally reserved for assassinations, the newspaper headline screamed:

POLICE HUNT DR. DOOM.

Chapter 14

CLASS WAS OVER; IT WAS SIX P.M. AS HANNAH crossed 14th Street toward the Seventh Avenue subway, page one of the *New York Post* caught her eye: POLICE HUNT DR. DOOM. Normally, she bought the *Times*, but as a single woman living alone. . . . Cursing herself for giving in to sensationalism, she handed the newsdealer a dollar, pocketed her change, and carried the *Post* down a flight of stairs to the subway platform. Only a few people were waiting, an indication that a train had just come and gone. Still, it was rush hour; the wait wouldn't be long. Ignoring the glance of a well-dressed man who passed by, Hannah opened the *Post* and began to read:

> New York City Police Department officials confirmed today that an all-out manhunt is underway for a psychotic killer who has murdered four women since April of this year. Each victim was an attractive single woman

143

living alone in Manhattan. The body of Elizabeth Wald, 30, was found in her apartment at 112 Hudson Street yesterday afternoon. Like the previous victims, Miss Wald had been stabbed to death by a single thrust to the carotid artery. Acknowledging the similarity of circumstances, Lieutenant Richard Marritt, who is in charge of the 50-man investigation, declared, "It takes a very powerful direct thrust to cut through the muscle that protects the artery. To kill with a single thrust on four separate occasions indicates strength, quickness, and a certain knowledge of anatomy."

Citing the surgical nature of the wounds, Marritt refused to rule out the possibility that the killer was a doctor or other health care professional. Meanwhile, an atmosphere of terror has fallen over single women in Manhattan. Police report—

"Hi! How are you?"

Hannah turned and saw Kyle beside her. For a moment, her thoughts blurred. Then, as quickly as they had gone, her surroundings returned.

"Kyle, leave me alone."

"Can't I even say hello?"

"And stop following me."

"I'm not following you. This is the subway I always take home."

Hannah stared at the tracks ahead, and said nothing.

"How was your day today?"

She didn't answer.

"I don't understand. Can't we have a civil conversation?"

Still no response.

"What is it with you?"

Other riders were filtering down the stairs onto the subway platform.

"All right, if that's the way you want it, I'll leave you alone. But let me ask one question. Did you get my novel?"

"Yes, Kyle, I got your novel. And I went to the post office yesterday to send it back to you."

"Did you like it?"

"No."

"I don't understand. What didn't you like?"

She should have told him she hadn't read it. Now there was another avenue for conversation.

"I mean, I respect your judgment. What didn't you like about it?"

"What I didn't like was finding myself in your novel."

"What do you mean?"

Why didn't the train come? Please, let there be a train.

"What do you mean, finding yourself in my novel?"

"Come off it, Kyle. I read the manuscript. Helen's clothes, her friends, what she does, everything about her. It's me, and I don't appreciate the invasion of privacy."

"I don't know what you're talking about."

"Fine, then we have nothing more to say to each other."

"I mean, I'm interested. I tried to make Helen a universal woman, someone all women could identify with. So if you identified with her, I guess that's good."

Off in the distance, Hannah could see a train coming.

"Why can't you just be civil and talk to me?"

"I don't want to talk anymore."

"But you have to. You don't understand. You're too special for me to let you pass by."

Hannah stepped back, away from the edge of the subway platform.

"That's why I called. That's why I invited you for dinner last month. Don't you understand? Twenty years ago I used to walk to school pretending I was walking with you. I've never—" The roar of the train drowned out the rest of the sentence. "You have to see me."

The subway doors opened. Hannah bolted, ten yards down the platform to the next car.

Cracked windows; graffiti on the walls; people jammed in like sardines in a can; safety in numbers. Kyle couldn't get to her.

Penn Station . . . Times Square. . . . The train rumbled on, snaking through darkened tunnels. Christ! What a lunatic. How can I get rid of him? How many men have had obsessive crushes on women? John Hinckley, for one. That's different. Hinckley never knew Jodie Foster. What about men who know women from work, or through a friend, or living in the same building, or school? Hannah had never imagined anyone as desperate for contact as Kyle—positive, negative, any kind. What can I do about him?

The subway slowed, then came to a halt at the 72nd Street station. Hannah got off. Ten yards ahead, Kyle stood waiting.

"Leave me alone! Get away or I'll scream."

"I'm changing trains, okay? I transfer to the local here."

"Then stay here, on the platform. If you follow me out, I'll call the police."

"You're crazy. Do you know that?"

Hannah turned on her heel and half walked, half ran down the subway platform, up the stairs, out onto Broadway. The early-evening air was warm, the sky streaked with orange and gold. Get hold of yourself. It's over. Concentrate on something else—anything— what you'll have for dinner tonight; he's

gone. West End Avenue . . . 71st Street . . .
70th. . . . That's better. She was starting to
think more rationally. *Why is Kyle doing
this? He must hate me. That's it; that's what
it is. But what happens to quiet anger like
this? Where does it go?*

Hannah's thoughts were growing more tied
to specific events and moments now. *Why
had Kyle sent a letter instead of just arrang-
ing to run into her on the street a month
ago? Think! Maybe he wanted time, two or
three hours together to make a good impres-
sion. All right, that was logical. Next question: Why did he choose now to confess his
love? Probably he decided he couldn't live
without me. That was possible; a warped
mind might think that way. But that didn't
explain the fact that he could have called,
pursued her, and still not confessed. Something was missing. Look at it from another
viewpoint. Maybe something had changed in
Kyle's life around the time he called. When
was it? A month ago. What was happening?
What was happening? . . . When was it? He
called . . . a month ago; there was a rose.
Kyle sent the roses; I know that. But the first
rose was in April, and he called in June.
There was a rose in April, and one in June,
and one right after the Fourth of July. And
let's not get carried away with this, but
women were being murdered in April, June,
and right around the Fourth of July.*

148

Hannah stepped into the vestibule of her apartment building, opened the mailbox, and reached for the note inside: "See super for package."

He was a nice man, the superintendent, Dominic Calamari. He'd lived in the building for thirty years. More than once he'd told Hannah about arriving with his parents in America in 1927; how on a cold winter morning his boat had steamed past the Statue of Liberty and docked at a pier on Ellis Island.

Hannah went down to the superintendent's basement apartment, thanked him for the package, and brought it upstairs. Parcel post; postmarked one day earlier. At least the mail moved swiftly, she told herself. "That's good, Banana," Fergy would have told her. "Keep your sense of humor. You'll need it."

Inside her apartment, she tore at the brown paper wrapper. There was a box ... and the stem and withered leaves of a headless rose ... and a card, the same as before: *THHIRWRDNK.*

Maybe denial was the best way to deal with reality. Besides, Hannah told herself, she was exaggerating and this was all a horrible fantasy, nothing more. Trembling, Hannah crumpled the wrapping paper, box, card, and rose into a ball, brought it out

149

into the hallway to the incinerator, and threw it down.

Kyle was gone now. He'd sent his novel and been rebuffed once and for all. She didn't want to think about him anymore.

Chapter 15

FERGY WAS IN WASHINGTON, D.C., FOR A CON-
ference the day Hannah had her subway-
platform confrontation with Kyle. The following morning he telephoned to say he was
home. "The trip was awful," he reported.
"Going down on the shuttle, there was a
baby that screamed the entire flight. I wanted
to stuff it in an overhead luggage compart-
ment, but the parents objected."

"And the conference?"

"Worse than the flight. I spent nine hours
sucking up to a pain-in-the-ass bureaucrat
who looked like a giant earthworm and has
the power to give us twelve million dollars
for an industrial park in the South Bronx. The
hotel I stayed in was crummy. The people in
the next room practiced bowling all night.
And this morning I read in the newspapers
that a psychopath named Dr. Doom is going
to make it impossible for me to pick up
women in New York."

"If it's any consolation," Hannah told him, "you aren't the only one with problems."

Whereupon she poured forth a detailed account of the previous day's encounter with Kyle.

"Maybe he's gathering material for a new novel," Fergy suggested.

"Thanks." There was a pause as Hannah debated whether to broach a subject that had been troubling her for the past twenty-four hours. "Fergy, I know this is crazy, but let me ask you something. Four women have been murdered—one in April, one in June, and two this month. Kyle sent roses in April, June, and twice in July. I don't want to let my imagination—"

"Banana," he interrupted. "You've been watching too many late-night movies on television."

It was the answer she wanted, but still she wasn't fully convinced. "How can you be sure?"

"Because I don't think the roses really coincided with the murders. You're imagining the timing to give yourself fits."

"No, I'm not."

"Sure, you are. Kyle is sick. His fantasies are so far from reality that he's guaranteed to have a breakdown unless he gets help, but nothing he's said or done indicates violence. And I'm not just saying that to make you feel

152

better. You're the best friend I have. I'd die if anything happened to you. I just don't think Kyle is dangerous."

Probably, Fergy was right, Hannah decided. She hadn't really kept track of when she'd gotten the roses. And Kyle was nonphysical, passive, even weak. Still, it troubled her to realize how long he'd been a shadow in her life. In retrospect it seemed that, in high school, Kyle had always sat one row behind her and one row to the left or right—perfect position for watching her in class. And she'd read his manuscript. Combine that with his calls, his letters, his confession of "love" —and something more than discomfort was at stake. He was a threat, and one exigency was particularly troubling. Up until now, Kyle had held onto the hope, maybe even the belief, that things between Hannah and himself would work out for the best. She wondered how he'd react when he realized that there wasn't any hope.

□ □ □

Richard Marritt stepped back from the map and surveyed his handiwork. Blue for Ethel Purcell; green for Linda Taylor; brown for Alison Schoenfeld. Now there was yellow— a thin yellow line that traced Elizabeth Wald's movements on the day she'd been murdered. Her Sunday had begun in lower Manhattan.

Brunch with a friend, a walk, then she'd gone alone to the Museum of Modern Art on West 53rd Street. There, the detective surmised, she had met her killer. Probably, he'd brought her home and been invited inside the apartment. After that. . . . Marritt's mind turned to the grim scene that had become too familiar. A fully clothed body; blood splattered on the furniture and floor. He wondered how many more colors would line the map on his office wall before summer was gone.

It was two P.M. The *Daily News* and *Post* were having a field day with the murders. Homicide makes for good press if a newspaper's readers identify with the victim. What better way to sell papers than by warning every woman in Manhattan that her life was in danger. The *Post* in particular was playing up the "no one is safe" angle. IT'S DR. DOOM'S MOVE read the headline in solid block letters. The *News* was slightly more restrained, but not by much. The result had been a flood of confessions and nut notes to police headquarters. Every letter, no matter how frivolous, would be checked for fingerprints. Each time a tip was telephoned in, the call was taped and, if possible, traced. Every scrap of information had been fed into the police computer to form a comprehensive data base. Maybe something would turn up—the same name in several murder victims' datebooks, a suspect who attended too many funerals. But unless and until something clicked, the investigation was floundering. All Marritt could do was study and restudy photographs of the murder sites, listen to messages left on Elizabeth Wald's telephone answering machine, catalogue objects found in the victims' apartments, and ask himself whether there was a pattern to the murder dates or any relevance to the fact that the last two victims had red hair.

The telephone rang and Marritt picked up the receiver, simultaneous with Dema entering his office. Gesturing for the younger cop to sit, the detective reached for a pad and began taking notes. "How many?" Dema heard him query. "All right, put them on the list. . . . That's right, low priority, but you never know."

"Just a hunch," Marritt told his partner after hanging up. "I figure we should get the names of everyone between age twenty and fifty who attempts suicide. It's a long shot, but maybe this guy will come to his senses and try to kill himself."

"Wishful thinking."

"Probably, but I got to think something to keep my spirits up. What else can I tell myself? Four women are dead. The autopsy reports read like carbon copies. There are no witnesses. And if we catch this guy, he'll probably get off by pleading insanity."

"No jury would buy it."

"Why not? The guy is crazy. Most people fantasize about murder at one time or another, but this guy does it. It's like with Bernhard Goetz. Thousands of New Yorkers dream about doing what Goetz did, but they don't. Goetz went out, got a gun, and shot four people. Only someone a little off his rocker would do that. Well, Dr. Doom, or whatever his name is, is a lot off his rocker. He functions; he has a job; he goes to work; but he's nuts." Wearily, the detective stared at the fingerprint card on the corner of his desk. "You know something?" he said, looking back toward Dema. "I'd give a year's salary to get this guy before he kills again. Every time I'm involved in a case like this, it turns personal for me. That's wrong; a cop shouldn't think like that. But I look at pictures of those four women, and it drives me up a wall. They could be my wife or kids. You can't stop something until it starts, but now that this guy has started killing people, as long as he's out there, I figure he's my responsibility."

"Not yours. Other people made him what he is, his parents, teachers—everyone who touched him."

"Maybe, but they're not around anymore. Or if they are, they aren't helping. Right now it's him and us, and he's winning. He's smart; he has good judgment when it comes to risks. I guess he's figured out how easy it is to get away with murder."

□ □ □

It was seven P.M. The television was broken. Not that it mattered; there wasn't much on worth watching anyway. Kyle sat alone on the bed in his apartment. Twenty-four hours had passed since his humiliation on the subway platform. Maybe tonight Hannah would come to her senses and call. How could she do that to me? It was awful. If I thought I could find someone else I love as much, I'd walk away from her. But I can't; not now, not ever. There's no one else like her.

Several magazines lay scattered on the floor—*Harper's, New York, Atlantic Monthly.* Reaching for the one closest to the bed, Kyle began turning pages. . . "Theater" . . . "Art" . . . . If another woman were here, I could close my eyes and pretend it was Hannah, but it wouldn't work. The other woman would talk and do things differently. More page turning . . . "Dance" . . . "Music" . . . "Strictly Personals" . . . I'll read the personals, just for fun—"Zaftig brunette" . . . "Charming Catholic woman" . . . Keep going . . . "Late 40's, classy" . . . No good; none of them.

BEAUTIFUL BLOND WRITER—Tall, slender, well-educated, very sexy authoress. Seeking my male counterpart: warm, intelligent, mid-30's. Box 702.

She might be good.

I wouldn't do this, not at all, except for what happened yesterday. It would be a way of taking Hannah off her pedestal. And if I do this right, Hannah would come crying and beg me to choose her.

"Dear Box 702." What should I write? "I'm adopted." No good. Start it over. "Dear Box 702. I remember when my parents gave me my first set of electric trains." That's better. It's creative and sets me off from the rest:

Dear Box 702,

I remember when my parents gave me my first set of electric trains. It was Christmas 1956, and those trains were far more important to me than Ike, Elvis, or Don Larsen's World Series perfect game.

Anyway, now that I've got your attention—I'm tall, slender, well-educated (Williams), and thirty-six years old. Like you, I'm an author. Could we meet for a drink, or maybe dinner?

I can't fall in love with somebody else; I'm in love with Hannah.

158

Crumple up the letter. Throw it in the wastepaper basket. I want to be faithful to Hannah. . . . "Beautiful blond writer—tall, slender, very sexy; intelligent, warm." Maybe she and Hannah together. . . . No! Keep them apart. If I had to choose, I'd choose Hannah. But if this woman. . . . At least seeing her might be good. And when Hannah comes back, I can choose Hannah. I shouldn't have crumpled up the letter. Now I have to rewrite it. I hope Hannah doesn't find out; not until she sees us and is jealous because we're together.

Hannah Wade, Hannah Wade
You're the prettiest girl God ever made

□ □ □

Fergy was asleep when the telephone rang.
"Hi! It's Hannah. Did I wake you up?"
Long silence.
"I guess I did. I'm sorry. I really just called to say good night."
"What time is it?"
"Around midnight. All I wanted was to thank you for everything you've done for me lately."
Again, there was silence.
"Hey, Fergy, are you all right?"
"I think so. It's just, I was having a really weird dream."
"Okay, go back to sleep."

Chapter 16

THE DAYS BLURRED FOR HANNAH. GIVEN THE nature of life as an artist, the distinction between weekday and weekend didn't really matter. She saw a movie, went to a concert, and dropped in on a party her neighbors were giving. All the guests seemed to have been created by Charles Dickens, with strange personalities and odd looks to match. She taught. She read. On a Monday night, two thirds of the way through July, she had dinner with Fergy.

They chose Metropolis, one of the newer additions to Restaurant Row on Columbus Avenue. Two dozen tables were comfortably spaced in a large atrium on a century-old tile floor. Wrought-iron columns painted white rose to the ceiling. There was quiet lighting, considerable greenery, and an open rotisserie at the west end of the room.

"How was your weekend?" Hannah queried when they'd been seated.

Fergy shrugged. "The same. Friday night I

had dinner with someone I met in the supermarket three months ago. Cute, blue eyes,
lots of blond hair. Getting the date was like
signing up for the New York City Marathon. I
had to fill out an entry form weeks in
advance."

"And?"

"There was a problem with age. She says
she's in tenth grade, but I think she's lying.
Ninth seems more like it. . . . Just kidding,"
he added, taking note of the look in Hannah's
eyes. "Actually, she's twenty-one, which is
still too young. How can I go out with
someone who wasn't alive when the Beatles
were on *The Ed Sullivan Show*? Anyway, that
was Friday. Saturday, I went to the movies
with a newly appointed vice-president from
Merrill Lynch, which was a colossal blunder.
Some men keep lists of women they've slept
with. This woman keeps files."

"What?"

"You heard me—files! For each guy she
goes out with, she writes down his name, a
summary of the date, and miscellaneous biographical data. Then, if they have inter-
course, she records the time, place, sexual
position, number of orgasms, and the guy's
sexual peculiarities."

"You're making this up."

"No, I'm not. I swear it. She showed me
her files."

A waiter appeared and handed them each an oversized white menu. Fergy ordered a vodka martini; Hannah, a Bloody Mary.

"And are you in her files?"

"As a date, yes. As a sexual partner, negative. Early in the evening she explained that she doesn't sleep with men who earn less than eighty thousand dollars a year."

"Why eighty thousand?"

"I have no idea. All I know is, she spent most of the evening talking about whether or not allowance for funds used during construction was properly capitalized as an item of other income on the consolidated balance sheet of a public utility that Merrill Lynch is financing. I would have been better off staying home and watching television."

The waiter returned, put their drinks on the table, and waited while they considered the menu.

"Sunday was even more momentous," Fergy continued after he and Hannah had given their orders. "I went to bed with an account executive from J. Walter Thompson whose primary virtue, forgive me, was that her breasts are so large she can touch her nipples together. This woman speaks of the man she hopes to find and marry the way Jews in ancient Egypt spoke of the Messiah. Her idea of heavy sex was to spit in my ear, and all night long she kept calling me sweetie, which

163

I hate. After we made love, I looked at her"—Fergy's voice faltered slightly, then picked up—"I looked at her, and wanted to snap my fingers and go poof to make her disappear. Actually, though, it was a learning experience. She has the shortest hair of any woman I've ever dated, and she'd be great for a married man who wanted an affair on the side. There'd be no strands of long hair for his wife to find on suits or around the apartment."

Hannah sat silent, weighing her response. Part of her liked it that Fergy was open with her, that he talked about sex and other women. In some ways, it even provided a sexual buffer between them; if they talked about other women, then surely the two of them would remain "just friends." And maybe, in a convoluted sort of way, the conversations afforded her a sexual outlet as well. But despite his jaunty retelling of events, Fergy seemed at the moment to be projecting an aura of considerable sadness.

"Do you know what your problem is?" she said at last. "You're hung up on sex and women's looks."

"Not true. No one says I have to marry the most beautiful woman in the world. Number two would do nicely."

"Be serious, Fergy. I'm your friend. I want to help. I'm not making judgments about normal or healthy or right and wrong. All I'm

looking at is what will make you happy. I've
been where you are. I've slept with men I'm
ashamed of sleeping with. A couple of times—
and they were bad times—I had to think to
remember the name of the man I was in bed
with. I've demanded standards in other people that I wasn't willing to meet myself, and
now I see you making the same mistakes."

"Maybe, but it's not exactly easy to get
everything right, Banana. You're an example
of that. You're bright; you're beautiful; you're
sexy; you're fantastic. You know all the right
mantras about joy and sharing and life and
love. But be honest. Why is it that, every time
you meet a man, you put a big *X* through his
name before you even get to know him?
You're just as guilty as I am of telling little lies
and not laying things on the table where they
belong. If I could find a good relationship—"

"You don't find a relationship," Hannah
corrected. "You build one."

"Then with all due respect, if you're so
smart, how come you haven't?"

It was a standoff.

The maître d' walked by with another
couple, whom he seated at a table nearby. The
man looked like Billy Joel. Hannah sipped
slowly at her Bloody Mary. Fergy finished his
vodka martini and ordered another. It was a
good time to change subjects.

"Kyle sent me another card," Hannah
offered.

"When?"

"It came in the mail this morning." Reaching for her purse, she drew out a Hallmark greeting card with a purple orchid sketched on the outside. "Here."

Fergy opened it up and looked at the message, penned in ink inside:

> Beside the garden wall when stars
>   are bright
> You are in my arms
> The nightingale tells his fairy tale
> Of paradise where roses grew
>
> > Love,
> > Kyle

"He's sort of a nut, isn't he?"

Hannah nodded.

"I guess he likes Hoagy Carmichael." Again, Fergy scanned the card. "Look at the way Kyle signed his name. The *k* is lower case."

The waiter returned and reached between them with their dinner entrees. Fergy finished his second drink. Hannah's grilled salmon looked magnificent.

"After the card came," Hannah said, resuming their conversation, "I did something silly."

"What was that?"

"I called the police. All this stuff about Dr. Doom and Kyle and dead roses in the mail was making me nervous, so this afternoon I telephoned the Dr. Doom hotline number."

"And?"

"Not much happened. A policeman answered, and I told him I'd gotten four dead roses—one after each killing—and I thought they'd come from a guy named Kyle Howard who's been obsessed with me for eighteen years. The cop asked for the exact dates I'd gotten the roses, and I couldn't remember. Then he asked if Kyle had broken any law, been violent, or made threats, and I told him no. By then, it was obvious the cop wasn't taking me seriously, and I started to feel pretty stupid. I gave him Kyle's address and telephone number. He thanked me, and that was it."

"Did he say whether or not they'd investigate further?"

"I gathered not."

Fergy sat back, a pensive look on his face. "It's strange," he said. "Ever since Kyle surfaced in your life, I've been reliving high school memories. When I was in eleventh grade, a black family moved into the district. One of their kids was my age, six feet four inches tall, the first black student ever to attend Jackson High, and he didn't know how to play basketball. The entire student body was heartbroken."

"Is that all you remember?"

"Of course not. But I keep wondering what

sort of memories Kyle has, and what keeps him from letting go of them. You'd think that, somewhere along the line, he'd have realized it was in his best interests to change—to seek professional help, do something to ease the pain."

"Maybe, but it hasn't happened, and I keep worrying about another option."

"What's that?"

"That Kyle might take all his rage and frustration and despair and pain, and turn them against me."

□　□　□

The apartment was depressing. It was his; it was lonely. It would be a much happier place if Hannah were there. She could move in with him, but actually her apartment was nicer; cozy, blissful. At least it had seemed that way the night he'd been there for coffee after dinner. How long ago had it been? Four weeks exactly.

What time is it? Just before nine at night. Staring at the telephone, Kyle waited. Maybe she'll call. She might tonight. If Hannah calls, I'll tell her she's been the formative influence in my life. I'll put it in those words; she'll have to listen. Dinner wasn't very good this evening: hamburgers, McDonald's. Maybe I should turn the phone off; sit here and just think for a day or two; not eat; clear my mind a little. It wouldn't matter. My mind is clear. It's funny, sometimes, the way things work out. When Hannah got married, I didn't think I could stand the pain. And then her divorce—exhilaration! Someday, when this is over, we'll look back and laugh together. *Forsan et haec olim meminisse juvabit.* I wonder how many people know that. *The Aeneid.* After the fall of Troy, Aeneas and his men were adrift at sea, enduring near-endless suffering. There was a shipwreck, and they were marooned on a deserted island. It was cold; there was a storm. They were weak and hungry. And Aeneas gathered his men together and told them, *"Forsan et haec olim meminisse juvabit"*—perhaps someday it will be pleasing to remember these things.

The jangle of the telephone broke into Kyle's wandering.

"Hello?"

"Hello, is this Kyle Howard?"

"Who is this?"

"My name is Liz Gutner. I got your letter this morning." There was a pause. *"New York* magazine—the personals column."

What day was it? Monday. He hadn't expected anything to happen this quickly.

"It was a great letter," the voice added. "I've done personals before, and most of the responses are pretty tacky. I can't tell you how many people send back Xeroxed letters. I mean, how can you believe someone who

169

tells you they've read your ad and they
fervently believe you have an amazing amount
in common when even their signature is
Xeroxed?"

"Right. I guess that's not very personal, is it?"

"No way. But your letter was great, especially the part about Ike and Elvis and the
electric trains. Anyway, I thought I'd call to
see if the invitation was still open for dinner."

"All right, when's good for you?"

"Well, it's only nine, and my plans for this
evening fell through. How about tonight?"

"Okay—except, I've eaten already. But we
could meet for a drink."

"How about someplace nice, like the cocktail lounge at the Gulf & Western Building,
the forty-third floor—Top of the Park."

"Sure. I mean, I'm wearing brown slacks
and a shirt. What will you be dressed like?"

"Don't worry, we'll find each other. I'll
leave now and be there by nine-thirty."

Kyle stepped off the elevator onto the forty-
third floor of the Gulf & Western Building at
nine twenty-nine. The cocktail lounge was half
empty. Plate glass windows dominated the
north and west walls, looking out on an extraordinary view. The George Washington Bridge,
northern Manhattan, Central Park, the Hudson
River and New Jersey—all sparkling in the
summer night. Adjusting his eyes to the muted
light, Kyle looked around. People were sitting

in small groups at round tables scattered across
the room. There were no single women in
sight.

I should probably wait by the entrance to
the lounge. That's better than getting a table;
at least, I think it is.

"Can I help you, sir?"

Kyle turned toward the hostess, a woman
in her mid-thirties who offered a professional
smile.

"No, thanks, I'm waiting for someone."

The hostess left.

Tall blond writer, beautiful, very sexy. Liz
Gutner is a funny name; it sounds Jewish.
Not that it matters, except how many Jewish
women are there with blond hair? Probably
it's dirty blond or strawberry.

An attractive dark-haired woman stepped
off the elevator and walked toward him.
She's pretty; I wonder if that's her. Eye
contact. The woman smiled and walked on
into the lounge, joining two men and a
woman who were already seated. Of course
it's not her. The hair color is wrong.

Maybe we'll really hit it off. Liz chose a
nice place; it's very romantic. Warm, well-
educated, stunning, slender blonde. If Hannah saw us together, she'd probably be jealous.
What time is it? Nine-forty. Probably Liz had
trouble getting a cab or something.

The elevator opened, and a middle-aged
couple stepped off.

Nine forty-five; nine-fifty. This really is very nice here. I wonder how much drinks cost. I have enough money, but still. If drinks are four dollars each, then there's tip and tax. Two drinks for each of us could be twenty dollars. It's worth it, though, if it turns out right. I wonder what she looks like. Cybill Shepherd would be good, except I'd like it if her hair was longer and there was more warmth in her face. Maybe she'll be someone like Helen in my novel, someone—

"Excuse me. Are you Kyle?"

Silence.

"You must be Kyle. I'm Liz. It's nice to meet you."

She was standing there, directly in front of him. Beautiful blond writer; tall, slender, well educated, very sexy. Except she wasn't. Her face had a hard, pinched-in look. Even in the dark, her hair—dyed blond—showed dark roots. She was wearing a leather miniskirt and metallic-looking blouse. She was forty, easily, and had never been pretty except in her imagination.

"Hi, I guess, I mean I didn't recognize you. The ad said you were tall."

She was short, too. Five-two, maybe a shade taller.

"Oh, that!" She smiled. "I put that in because once, when I did a personals, one of my friends recognized me from the ad and really teased me."

The hostess came and led them to a table in the center of the room. Liz took out a cigarette and lit it.

"I liked your letter. I told you that already. What was it that made you write me?"

And her makeup. She was wearing too much makeup. Heavy lip liner, dark eye shadow. She's talking to me. Answer her.

"I don't know. I guess, I'm a writer and you said you're a writer too. You sounded nice."

"It was hard, figuring out what to write for the advertisement. I wanted to make myself sound attractive, but I didn't want to exaggerate. I guess you tried to do the same thing with your letter."

A waiter came and took their drink orders.

Why did the hostess have to put us in the center of the room where everyone can see us? She looks like a whore.

"You said in your letter that you went to Williams and you're a writer. What sort of writing do you do for a living?"

"I'm a novelist."

"Can you support yourself doing that?"

"Pretty much so," Kyle answered. "Sometimes I supplement my income by writing articles."

There was no harm in lying.

"Would I have read any of your books?"

Her teeth had a yellow cast from smoking too much. One of the front ones was jagged.

"I said, would I have read any of your books?"

"Probably not."

Just leave me alone. I wish it were over.

The waiter returned with their drinks and a small bowl of peanuts.

"Are you all right?" Liz queried. "You seem kind of distant."

"I'm fine. It's just, I'm sort of preoccupied at the moment. Not long ago I broke up with a woman I was going out with. She's someone I dated a long time ago in high school. I should have married her then, but I wasn't mature enough."

"At seventeen?"

"Probably. Anyway, after we broke up, when we were younger, I went out with a lot of different people. Then, not too long ago, we got back together but it didn't work. I mean, she's still interested but it's not the same. Anyway, I just thought it was only fair to tell you I'm sort of involved with someone."

Liz Gutner's eyes homed in like radar. "I guess you're saying you don't like the way I look."

"No! I mean, I think you're very nice-looking."

"Well, you're not perfect either, and I'm getting ticked off. I got all dressed up. I came all the way up here from Twentieth Street and First Avenue, and you haven't even asked

174

what I do for a living. All you did was take one look and write me off."

"That's not true. I like you. I'm just trying to be honest."

"Bullshit, you're trying to be honest. I've had it up the wazoo with guys like you. All you care about is blond hair and tits. Well, you know something? I'm not any happier being here right now than you are. But I'll tell you something else. I'm going to sit at this table and finish my drink because it's pretty here and I like the view. And you're going to sit with me until I'm done, and then you can go home and call your goddamned high school sweetheart."

□ □ □

Eleven P.M. The same night.

Hannah stood at the edge of her bed and turned down the covers. Her left knee ached at the point where cartilage and tendon joined together. An occupational hazard. Dancers' turnouts caused more knee problems than middle linebackers ever suffered, but aches like this dissolved with an evening's rest.

It had been a nice night. She always had a good time when she was with Fergy. She was never bored and almost always happy when they were together.

The air was warm. July in the city. Shadows from the street reached across the bed-

175

room. Maybe Fergy was right. Maybe she did cross people off a little too quickly. For example, looking at it objectively, what was wrong with Fergy?

The question surprised her. Not that she couldn't come up with a workable answer. Simply put—

The telephone rang. . . . Once . . . twice. . . . Reaching across her bed, Hannah picked up the receiver.

"Hi! This is Kyle."

The sound of his voice reverberated in her head like an automobile theft-alarm siren.

"I know it's late, but I had to talk with you."

"Kyle, I thought you understood, I don't want to talk with you anymore."

"I know, but you have to listen. All my life, I've been lonely. The only happiness I know is you."

"That's not my problem."

"But all I want is to be with you. In high school, all the time, I imagined our being together. Every dance, every event, I fantasized being with you. I can't even begin to tell you how many times I've walked down the street pretending I'm with you, or that you'll come up behind me and take my hand."

The bedroom seemed to be growing darker, with Kyle's disembodied voice coming out of the night.

"Hannah, you have to understand. No one

has ever hurt me as much as you. And no one could ever make me happier. Please! Just talk to me."

"Kyle, I'm sorry. I'm not your shrink."

"Please! Just talk to me, just for a minute. Don't hang up. All I'm—"

Click.

◻ ◻ ◻

The problem with going to law school was, when you got out, you were a lawyer. At least, after five years on Wall Street, that was how Susan Marino viewed the matter. The work was dull, the atmosphere oppressive, and the hours deadly. Take tonight, for example. Susan had been at her desk poring over documents until 11:10 P.M. Dial-A-Cab hadn't picked her up until 11:30, and, on the way home, she'd realized that (a) she was hungry and (b) there was no food in her refrigerator. Ergo, she'd asked the driver to drop her off at the twenty-four-hour supermarket two blocks from her apartment. Once there, Susan decided she might as well shop for the week. Milk, juice, bread, cheese. It began to mount up. Plus there were some bulky items like paper towels and three rolls of toilet paper. It came to forty-three dollars and six cents (which wasn't a problem) and filled two shopping bags (which was—because Susan was also carrying her attaché case, it was too late for delivery service, and she wasn't the strongest person in the world). Fumbling with her bags and attaché case, she made it out of the supermarket as far as the curb. That was when the guy who'd been on line behind her and was carrying a single quart of orange juice offered to help. He seemed nice; soft-spoken; five feet ten inches tall, maybe a shade taller. In his mid-thirties with pleasant features and brown hair. Walking the two blocks to her apartment, they made the necessary introductions—Susan Marino, Arnold Tinsley. And then Susan did something stupid. She invited him upstairs for a cheese sandwich. Even at the time, she'd known it was dumb; but she was lonely and wanted to talk to someone while she ate, and it was too late to call any of her friends for company. Besides, Susan prided herself on being a good judge of character. She always guessed right.

The trouble started inside her apartment. At first, everything was copacetic. They discussed politics and social issues of the late 1960s. "Where did all that idealism go?" Arnold wondered. "The students graduated and got jobs," Susan had answered. By then they were eating their cheese sandwiches. "Most people don't know if they were breast fed or bottle fed," Arnold offered. The comment was disjointed, totally unconnected to what they'd been talking about. Susan wasn't sure whether to respond or ignore it. What she did in the end was smile and eat her cheese sandwich a little more quickly.

"I have a friend who's a dancer," Arnold told her. "Try walking on the points of your toes sometime, just for a minute. It hurts like hell, and it's almost impossible to maintain your balance."

It was sort of sad, actually, watching her shovel her cheese sandwich into her mouth, trying to finish it so she could throw him out. There was a piece of food—a caraway seed or something—lodged between his teeth. Maybe Susan would let him use her Water Pik.

"I don't have a Water Pik," she answered.

"Maybe a toothpick or something?"

"I'm afraid I don't have a toothpick, either."

That was when he'd taken out the knife. And Susan considered screaming, but decided her chances were better if she didn't.

"Actually, my name isn't really Arnold Tinsley," he told her.

"I don't understand."

"Arnold is just the bad boy I created inside me. Do you give blow jobs?"

"Arnold, please . . ."

"I just told you. My name isn't Arnold."

"All right, I'll call you anything, anything you want."

"My friends call me Fergy."

PART FOUR

Chapter 17

"LADIES AND GENTLEMEN, GOOD MORNING. I'M
Harvey Granfort, Chief of Detectives for the
New York City Police Department. The gen-
tleman to my left is Lieutenant Richard
Marritt. We're here because, yesterday afternoon, the body of a thirty-year-old attorney
named Susan Marino was found in her apartment at Three-oh-nine West Sixty-seventh
Street. The victim had been stabbed once in
the carotid artery. Her body was fully clothed
with no evidence of sexual molestation. Laboratory tests concluded earlier this morning
substantiate that fingerprints found in Miss
Marino's apartment are identical to those
found in the apartments of four previous
murder victims. This press conference is being
held to advise the public via the news media
regarding the status of the case. What I'd like
now is for Lieutenant Marritt, who's in charge
of the investigation, to take over the briefing."

As was the case eight days earlier, the
auditorium at One Police Plaza was jammed.

A half-dozen television cameras stood ready to roll. The lights seemed brighter than before, but Marritt figured maybe that was only his imagination.

"I'm not quite sure where to begin," the detective said, taking hold of the microphone. "As all of you know, between April eighteenth and July thirteenth of this year, four women were murdered in their apartments in Manhattan. Each of you is familiar with the modus operandi of the killer. Two days ago, on July twenty-first, he struck again. As best we can determine, Susan Marino worked until eleven P.M. on Monday night at her office on Wall Street. From there she took a radio cab to the Lincoln Supermarket, two blocks from her home. The supermarket checkout clerk remembers seeing her, and says the victim entered and left the supermarket alone. Her body was found at four P.M. yesterday afternoon. The time of death is estimated at one A.M.—that is, one hour after she left the supermarket. Evidence found in her apartment suggests that she and a second person, presumably the killer, were eating sandwiches at the time she was killed. This is confirmed by autopsy findings, which match the un-eaten portion of a sandwich found on Miss Marino's kitchen table with the undigested remains in her stomach and intestines."

A murmur swept the auditorium floor.

"I'm sorry to be so graphic," Marritt said,

responding to the sound. "But it's important that each and every one of you understand what's going on. As Chief Granfort indicated, fingerprints found in Miss Marino's apartment are identical to those found in the apartments of four previous murder victims. As of today, the number of detectives assigned to the case has been increased to seventy-five. Every possible lead is being pursued. If you have any questions, now's the time to ask them."

A flurry of hands shot into the air, as dozens of reporters shouted to be heard.

"Hold on," Marritt pleaded. "I can only answer one question at a time. Let's start with the genteman in the blue sweater over there."

For the next forty minutes, before a demanding, sometimes hostile press, the detective held his ground. "We're already using computers," he responded to one inquiry. "And so far it hasn't helped." . . . "As of now, we've examined one hundred thousand fingerprints without a match." . . . "The reason I haven't referred to the perpetrator as Dr. Doom is because, in my view, nicknames and labels of that nature simply increase the chance of a copycat killer." . . . "Yes, I'm aware of the statistics regarding crime in New York. You want statistics, I'll give you statistics. There are eighteen hundred murders committed in this city each year. Six percent are between family members; seventeen percent result from robberies; fifty percent are the result of arguments. Eighty-two percent of the victims and eighty-seven percent of the killers are men."

Slow down, Marritt told himself. Don't lose control.

"Sir, I wonder if you could tell us what the public can expect in the next week or two?"

Marritt took a deep breath and let it out in stages. "From the police department, the public can expect an all-out effort. We're very frustrated, but we're doing the best we can. From the perpetrator—" The detective paused, wondering whether to go on. "As far as the perpetrator is concerned, we're face to face with a very grim reality. The first victim, Ethel Purcell, was killed on April eighteenth of this year. Two months elapsed between that date and June seventeenth, when Linda Taylor was killed. Since then, the interval between homicides has been reduced to sixteen, ten, and now eight days. Those figures speak for themselves."

After the press conference, Marritt returned to the precinct house where a dozen "please call" messages lay scattered on his desk. Answering the most important himself, he instructed Dema to handle the others, then checked his diary for the hours ahead. There was a meeting scheduled for two P.M. with a representative of the mayor's office and a four o'clock conference with a police psychiatrist who, hopefully, would be able to shed some light on how to stop "Dr. Doom."

A young cop came upstairs to the detective's office with special editions of the *New York Post* and *Daily News*. The *News* had run an extra printing with a front-page OPEN LETTER TO DR. DOOM. Not to be outdone, the *Post* was on the stands with a front-page plea: DR. DOOM: PLEASE GIVE UP. TURN YOURSELF IN TO THE POST SO THE CARNAGE WILL END.

Inside the *Post*, there were thumbnail sketches of "Dr. Doom's Five Victims" and extensive quotes from Susan Marino's coworkers and friends. "Police report a deluge of tips and no solid leads," the article concluded. "Members of the public with information that might be helpful in solving the murders should call 520-9200. Chief of Detectives Harvey Granfort has said that every available detective will be enlisted in the investigation. Reward money totaling $25,000 has been offered by various civic groups for information leading to the arrest and conviction of Dr. Doom."

At two P.M. Marritt conferred with the mayor's representative. Then, after a late lunch, he took a squad car to Tenth Avenue and 59th Street to meet with a police psychiatrist on the faculty at John Jay College of Criminal Justice. The college itself was located in a four-story, tan brick building that marked the end of one neighborhood and the beginning of another. To the south, drab industrial structures and a public housing project predominated. One block north, highrise buildings with $1,200-a-month studio apartments prevailed.

Dr. Herman Richardson's office was on the second floor. Marritt introduced himself and took a seat opposite the desk. Several minutes of small talk followed. Richardson was in his mid-forties, balding, with a pronounced birthmark beneath his left eye. When he spoke, he looked directly at Marritt, which the detective liked, but otherwise there was no hint regarding the psychiatrist's character. Then the conversation turned substantive.

"You know why I'm here," Marritt began. "Over the past three months, five women have been murdered. Each victim was stabbed once in the carotid artery, found fully clothed with no evidence of sexual molestation. There's never a sign of forced entry, and fingerprints indicate the same person was responsible for each death. That's it."

Richardson opened a file folder on top of his desk and reached for a pencil. "Naturally, I've read newspaper accounts and your own personal reports," he told the detective. "But let's make certain I have my facts right. How old were the victims?"

"They ranged in age from twenty-five to thirty-two."

"What did they look like?"

"Pleasant-looking but not beautiful. The tallest was Elizabeth Wald, about five-foot-seven. Alison Schoenfeld was the shortest—five-three, maybe a shade less. Ethel Purcell was fairly buxom; she was the first victim. Linda Taylor, the second, was flat-chested. Two of the women had red hair." The detective paused, groping for something more. "That's it. There's no common denominator—just five, relatively young, pleasant-looking women."

"Where in the apartments were their bodies found?"

"In the living room area. All except Susan Marino. She was in the kitchen."

"And I gather from your reports that there was evidence of social amenities. Drinks, a sandwich, things like that."

"Yes."

As the two men talked, Richardson began scribbling notes.

"What race were the victims?"

"White."

"And their jobs?"

"Susan Marino was a lawyer. As for the others, Elizabeth Wald was an artist, Alison Schoenfeld a social worker, Linda Taylor a secretary, and Ethel Purcell worked for a brokerage house."

"Were any of them dating anyone in particular?"

"Alison Schoenfeld had a boyfriend she saw fairly regularly. He was out of town that week."

"And, I take it, the killer left no notes."

"That's correct."

Richardson stopped writing. "Lieutenant, I don't want to intrude on your business—"

"Dr. Richardson, you can come as far into my business as you'd like. Right now I'm desperate for help."

The psychiatrist smiled. "I understand. What I started to say was, in cases of this nature, there's very little a psychiatrist can do to pinpoint the identity of the killer. All I can offer is a very rough, highly speculative profile, and even that might be off base. But let's start with a few basics. On the surface at least, the killer is likely to appear quite mild. Women trust him enough to invite him into their apartments, and these are well-educated, upper-middle-class women. That means he projects a relatively responsible and sophisticated aura to the average eye. The fury he harbors is well disguised. I'd guess he's between the ages of twenty-five and forty, possibly a bit older. The odds are that he's not very successful at what he does for a living. Successful people do commit murder, but generally not murders of this type. Most likely, he's lonely and lives alone. His life has

190

been filled with pain and suffering, but no one knows about it. He's the sort of person who finds it difficult to ask for help, and guards knowledge of his failure extremely well. He's average-looking, talks and dresses like a normal person, watches television, votes, reads magazines, and pays taxes. He gets to know his victims on a superficial level, and has the ability to establish at least superficial relationships. We know that because of his social interaction with the people he kills. Because of those relationships—and considering his modus operandi, which is almost antiseptic—I'm inclined to think he's not psychotic."

For the first time since Richardson began, Marritt interrupted. "How can someone who murders five women not be psychotic?"

"What I mean by that is, psychotics can't differentiate between fantasy and reality. For example, a psychotic might harbor the delusion that, with each murder, he's killing the Queen of the Night; or a psychotic might have a multiple personality and be totally unaware of what he's done. I doubt very much that this is the case with your killer. More likely, he's an extraordinarily compartmentalized individual who keeps the people and events in his life apart from each other. In between killings he's aware of his actions but trivializes the nature of what he's done. He has no conscience, feels no guilt, and is outside the most rudimentary fundamentals of societal control. To the extent he thinks about what he's done at all, he considers it justified. He probably believes he can stop at any time, turn over a new leaf, and the murderer in him will be gone."

"Can he really stop?"

"I doubt it."

Marritt sat silent, uncertain what to ask next. "But why? What made this person suddenly snap?"

"It's highly improbable that he suddenly snapped," Richardson answered. "More likely, it came after a long history of deprivation and disturbed behavior. The killer has a core of frightening rage, and since he's killing women, most likely that rage is directed at his mother. He lacks true adult emotions, leaving us with a preadolescent mind directing the actions of an adult behind a deadly facade. Chances are, he has a childlike concept of women as remote and unreal. On some level, he sees them as dangerous people, threats, which would allow him to perceive the murders as a form of self-defense, striking out before the women strike at him. Throughout his life, where pleasure is concerned, he's been an observer, not a participant. The sexual relations he's attempted with women have been failures or, to the degree successful, they've been stimulated by

violent fantasies. For all we know, every time
he has sex, he fantasizes that his penis is a
gun and, when he ejaculates, his sperm is the
equivalent of bullets shooting into a woman's
body. Regardless, this is a man who feels
profoundly inadequate, and murder is his
only means of compensation. Something inside him builds to the point where he feels
compelled to release it, but the murder solves
none of his problems, so he kills again."

Marritt waited until he was certain the psychiatrist was done, then began to question again.
"How far in advance does he plan the killings?"

"Maybe weeks, maybe hours. It's even possible that he's in apartments with a dozen
different women each month, and doesn't
decide to kill until the last moment. Either
way, the hunt for a victim gives him a feeling
of superiority, strength, and great power. It's
the equivalent of sexual foreplay, and the
killing is his orgasm."

"Does he get pleasure from the killings?"

"My guess is he does."

"And he's killing his mother?"

"Probably. Although at the time of the
killing, he sees a generic woman."

"What does that mean?"

"The victims are interchangeable. For killing purposes, one woman is as good as
another. It's a common phenomenon, really.
Many rapists who admit their crimes can't
even identify their victims."

"Is there any publicity we could disseminate through the media that might influence his actions?"

"Minimal publicity would probably be best. I doubt very much that you can reach this person with a positive message. Any attempt at manipulation will lead to escalation. For example, if you go public with a statement like 'We know you're suffering and we want to help you,' his most likely response will be to say 'fuck you' and go out to kill again."

Marritt leaned back, and stared at the psychiatrist. Everything was "most likely," "maybe," and "possibly," with nothing concrete for the detective to go on.

"There is one thing more," Richardson added.

"What's that?"

"Somewhere along the line, most serial murderers want credit for their actions. They write a note, develop a trademark, or do something in the nature of bragging. I know you've used computers, old-fashioned forensics, and everything else at your command, and come up with nothing. But my guess is, somehow, some way, this killer is sending a very pointed message to someone every time he commits a murder."

□ □ □

THHIRWRDNK

Hannah sat on her living room sofa and stared at the card.

Five murders. And now, headless rose number five had come in the mail. All the product of her imagination—that's what Fergy had told her, and with things like this, Fergy was usually right. Still, the withered stem and shriveled leaves weren't imaginary. The thorns were real. The box and brown wrapping paper were right in front of her.

On the living room floor, the newspaper headline screamed AN OPEN LETTER TO DR. DOOM. But the police weren't interested in roses. She'd already tried to enlist their aid to no avail. Bending over, Hannah gathered the box, the headless rose, and brown wrapping paper. She should throw them out, she decided. That was probably the best thing to do.

Walking down the corridor to the incinerator chute, she imagined Kyle lurking in the hall. He wasn't there, of course. That part, anyway, was her imagination, and it made her feel better, being able to tell herself she was only imagining things. But when she got back to her apartment, she looked down at the living room floor and the card was still there.

THHIRWRDNK.

Should she throw it out? Probably. But maybe the fact that she'd left it behind by accident on her first trip to the incinerator

195

was an omen. Keep it, Hannah told herself. Put it in the desk drawer with card number two from June. It was too bad, really, that she hadn't kept the other cards too. If she had, soon there might be enough for dinner place cards—an even dozen, maybe more.

Chapter 18

NEW YORK UNDER SIEGE.

TERROR SPREADS.

DR. DOOM 5; COPS 0.

Throughout the week, the headlines rolled on. Hannah tried to ignore them, but it was impossible. Even *The New York Times* put the murders on page one. She taught; she went to museums; she continued her daily routine as best she could and focused on little things— like how her mailman must feel, knowing that half the mail he delivered was junk mail that people discarded without even opening. And she thought about Kyle. He was in her life now, and she didn't know how to get rid of him.

Fergy telephoned late Thursday to report on a dinner with several staff members from the Manhattan borough president's office. "Technically, we were there to discuss the Forty-second Street Development Project," he told her. "But the real reason we got together

197

was that certain government officials wanted the taxpayers to buy them a lobster dinner."

"Where'd you go?"

"The Water Club, which was very good and very expensive. At least I'm getting something back for my tax dollars."

"Maybe next time you could discuss black voter registration at Lutèce."

"I doubt it. According to the major governmental luminary in attendance tonight, French food is too pompous. He had an escargot dinner once, and wasn't happy with it."

At the close of the conversation, they made plans for Sunday brunch. "I've got a big date Saturday night," Fergy told her. "If things go well, I'll give you a report."

Saturday, the mailman brought another card from Kyle:

> In my heart
> There is boundless love for you

Hannah didn't know whether to be scared or not. Her own personal disk jockey; Dick Clark incarnate. Maybe she should send him a card back with lyrics from Bob Dylan—"It Ain't Me, Babe."

Sunday at noon, she met Fergy at a neighborhood restaurant for brunch. Midway through the meal an attractive woman in her twenties came over to their table to say hello, and

Fergy introduced her to Hannah as "the one and only Peggy Norris."

"Who's Peggy Norris?" Hannah queried when the woman had left.

"A paraprofessional who works in my office; fairly bright, but on the manipulative side."

"She seemed nice," Hannah offered.

"That's because she was on good behavior. About a week ago, Peggy was talking about ballet and I told her about you."

"What did you say?"

"That you were my best friend, a fantastic dancer, and that I'm in love with you. Then I opined that anything you or Baryshnikov can do to music, Julius Erving can do with a basketball."

"You're impossible; you know that, don't you?"

"We're all imperfect."

After brunch they went for a walk in Riverside Park. The sky was gray, the temperature in the mid-sixties. For a while they talked about Woody Allen and Mia Farrow.

Then, gradually, the conversation turned more serious. "When I was ten, John Kennedy was elected President of the United States," Fergy offered. "I thought it would be great fun to change places with President Kennedy, but three years later he got shot. After that, I never wanted to be anyone else, but around the time I turned twenty, it did

199

occur to me that there would be certain advantages in trading places with John Lennon, assuming Yoko Ono wasn't part of the bargain. Then John Lennon got shot too, and I decided I was best off just being myself."

"That's not so bad, is it?"

"Not really. How about you, Banana? Did you ever want to be anyone else?"

"All the time, when I was little. My grandparents didn't want me. The only time I was happy was when I was dancing. I guess my best years were right after I came to New York, before I hurt my back. Marriage was awful. Getting divorced was a relief, but I can't say I was happy after that. As for now, there isn't anyone I'd like to change places with. I guess I don't really know what I want."

Reaching the northern end of the promenade, they turned south.

"Probably, childhood and marriage were the two worst periods in my life," Hannah continued. "People do certain things and you can never trust them again. That's what happened, first with my grandparents and then with my husband. Although I suppose you could say that my parents dying was the first betrayal, even though it wasn't their fault."

"Do you remember them?"

"Not my father. I remember my mother a

little, but not much. Somewhere along the line, I tried to put a protective covering over their absence. I told myself that their dying was something that happened to someone else, not to me, but inside I was never able to convince myself of that."

"You're still wonderful. You know that, don't you?"

Hannah smiled. "People tell me that from time to time. It's just—oh, shit! Over there—look!"

"What?"

"By the garden, at the end of the promenade. You've never seen him before, have you?"

"Seen who?"

"The one with the brown slacks. That's Kyle."

Fergy stopped and stared at the solitary figure standing by a bench where the promenade came to an end. Kyle was motionless, gazing with studied indifference toward the Hudson River but not really looking at what he saw.

"He's following us," Hannah said, lowering her voice so only Fergy could hear her.

"Are you sure?"

"Of course I'm sure. I'll prove it. Start walking, and Kyle will follow. Stop, and he'll stop too."

They began moving south, walking slowly, not looking back.

"This is crazy," Fergy told her. "Are you sure he's following?"

"Just give it another minute, then we'll look." Reaching a break in the cast-iron railing that ran along the promenade, they came to a halt. "All right," Hannah instructed. "Take a look."

Fergy turned. Kyle had moved in their direction, covering approximately the same distance they had, keeping the same space between them. Once again, he was gazing toward the river.

"Fergy, let's get out of here."

"Why? Because some nut is following us in the park?"

"Because I'm scared."

"I don't care. This is ridiculous." Taking her by the arm, he began to walk toward the spot where Kyle stood waiting.

"Fergy, what are you doing?"

"You'll see."

"Please! Be careful!"

"I'll be very careful."

"What are you doing?"

Fergy didn't answer. Instead he led her closer to Kyle, who maintained his gaze toward the Hudson River. The distance between them narrowed . . . Twenty yards . . . ten . . . five. . . . Kyle kept staring at the water. Finally, when they were too close for him to pretend he didn't see them any longer, he turned with mock surprise.

"Oh, hi!"

Hannah stood silent.

Fergy took one final step forward. "Excuse me. Are you Kyle?"

"Yes."

"All right. Kyle, I don't know what your problem is, and to be honest, I don't care. All I know is, Hannah is very upset by the fact that you're bothering her. I don't want you to send Hannah any more flowers. I don't want you to make any more telephone calls or write books about her. I don't want you to send any more cards or follow her around anymore. Leave Hannah alone."

"I don't know what you're talking about."

"You heard me. Leave Hannah alone."

"I don't know what you're talking about," Kyle repeated.

"I said, leave Hannah alone."

For an eternal second they faced one another, staring into each other's eyes. Then Kyle turned, and began to walk briskly away. Two steps . . . three. . . . And then Hannah heard the sound—a low awful choking sob that crescendoed to a tormented wail. And suddenly Kyle was crying out loud, running, actually physically running away.

"Oh, my God," she whispered.

Fergy looked on, stunned.

"Oh, my God. There's no telling what he'll do now."

Fergy groped for something, anything to

say. "The heart has its reasons which reason doesn't know."

"That's very poetic," Hannah countered. "But—"

A crack of thunder sounded above.

"Shit," she muttered. "It's going to rain."

□　□　□

Richard Marritt sat at his desk, dividing his attention between a pile of newspaper clippings and droplets of rain collecting on the windowsill. According to *The New York Times*, many violent criminals suffered from high levels of lead and cadmium and low levels of cobalt in their blood. There were also anomalies involving sodium, potassium, and copper, suggesting "a biological predisposition to violence."

"Whatever that means," the detective muttered.

Another article, dealing with progressive sex offenders, focused on "flashers": "Most exhibitionists have no intention of having sex with their victims," the article stated. "They expose themselves to prove they don't need women."

The office door opened, and Dema entered. "How's it going?"

"Life is a trauma," Marritt answered. Reaching into his back pocket, the detective took out a handkerchief that looked as though it hadn't been washed for eight months. "And

to tell the truth, I don't care if this is the last
murder I ever work. The next time a case like
this comes in, I hope I'm on Jupiter."

"That bad?"

Marritt nodded. "It's times like this that I
think everyone's crazy. Right now we're getting a dozen letters a day from people who
claim they're Dr. Doom. One nut says he's a
dentist who's strangled twelve people with
dental floss. Another genius sent a postcard
with two words underlined in purple—'guilt'
and 'toilet.' We're getting poems, nude photos, condoms with semen. If I ever decide to
stop being a cop, I can always be a psychiatrist. This job makes me an expert at dealing
with nuts."

Dema lowered himself into a chair opposite
the desk. Marritt blew hard into the handkerchief and returned it to his pocket.

"Anyway," the detective continued, "this
case is busting me up. Yesterday I figured
maybe we should print Dr. Doom's fingerprints in the newspapers and ask employers
to check their employees for a match, but the
ACLU would have a fit. Then I thought
maybe I should make a public plea—you
know, 'Dr. Doom, please give yourself up'
—but I'm not groveling for anybody, and
besides, the police psychiatrist said it wouldn't
work. Meanwhile, David and Jonathan think
I'm a hero because my name's in the newspapers all the time, except pretty soon they're

gonna start wondering why I can't catch this nut."

Dema waited.

"And unfortunately, lots of other people, mostly politicians, are wondering the same thing. Did you see the *Post*?"

The younger cop nodded.

"Why the governor is getting involved is beyond me. I used to be impressed by politicians. Once, about twenty years ago, I thought they were smart. Then I got assigned to guard Nelson Rockefeller for a day in the Bronx. Most of what he said was double-talk, and he must have had an upset stomach or something, because all day long he farted. After that, I wasn't in awe of Rockefeller or anyone else anymore."

The telephone rang, and Marritt picked up the receiver. "All right," Dema heard him grumble. "I'll be home at the latest by six o'clock."

"That was my wife," the detective said when the conversation was over. "Her Aunt Ellen is coming for dinner. I can't be late."

"At least it'll get you away from the office."

"Yeah, but what a price. Having Ellen for dinner is like having the flu for a week. Last year she visited China, and before every meal she pulled the waiter aside and asked him to tell the chef not to use monosodium glutamate." All of a sudden Marritt stood up. "Damn! This case is driving me nuts. Last night I tried telling myself I was blowing it out of proportion. People get killed in car crashes every day. I'm gonna die someday. My children will too—although that bothers me; I hope I'm not around to see it." His voice trailed off, then picked up again. "Anyway, I guess what bothers me is that this guy, Dr. Doom, probably hasn't done anything worthwhile in his entire life. And now he's grabbed onto the power over innocent people to determine life and death."

"The power of God," Dema murmured.

"The power of Satan is more like it."

□ □ □

It was ten o'clock. Fergy had just gone home for the night. Hannah sat alone in her bedroom, thinking back on the day's events. The day; the week; her life. After she and Fergy had gotten back to her apartment, coincidental with the rain, he'd asked if he could see her childhood photos. He'd been curious, that's all. And Hannah had been forced to tell him there weren't any, because her grandparents hadn't wanted her. Maybe we're all victims, she told herself now as she sat alone. Maybe that's the meaning of life. But there were degrees of victimization and degrees of suffering, and no matter what happened, no one should turn out like Kyle.

Kyle! There he was again, intruding in her mind.

The newspapers were full of stories about Dr. Doom. "A psychopath run amok is a marvelous killing machine," said an authority quoted by *The New York Times*. Jack the Ripper murdered seven prostitutes in the London slums at the end of the nineteenth century, another portion of the article noted. "It's a lousy way to die," the police commissioner opined regarding the victims at the end of the article.

Any way is a lousy way to die, Hannah decided. But at least a person should have a chance to live.

The telephone rang, probably Fergy calling to say good night. If everyone in the world were as good as Fergy, it would be a better place to live.

"Hello?"

"Hannah, this is Kyle."

Not again. "Kyle, I'm hanging—"

"Listen to me, Hannah. And listen good, because you'll never hear from me again."

"Wonderf—" she started to answer. But before she could finish, Kyle was talking again.

"I've taken pills. A lot of them. Enough to kill me. Because of you."

"Kyle, don't be so theatrical."

"And every time you fuck someone, for the rest of your life, you'll think of my dead body. That's my curse on you."

"Kyle, you're deranged."

"Yes, I'm deranged because everything is dead inside. I'm deranged because I've had a miserable lonely life, and all my life I've felt I could die and it wouldn't matter except for the things I wanted to say and do with you."

His words were beginning to slur together, growing harder to understand.

"All I wanted was to be with you. That's all I asked. Good-bye, Hannah. I love you."

Then the line went dead.

Hannah sat there, wondering what to do. It was a bluff; she knew that. But it had sounded real. And Kyle had hung up on her. He'd never done that before. Every other time, he'd kept talking to her as though his life depended on maintaining contact.

She wouldn't call him. That would be playing right into his hands. It would allow him to manipulate her even more. Besides, what if Kyle really had taken pills? She'd be better off if he was dead. That was the end of it. That was all. But then guilt started to work its way. If Kyle really had tried to commit suicide, Hannah reasoned, calling the police was the right thing to do. And if he hadn't, he deserved all the embarrassment in the world. So around midnight, Hannah picked up the telephone and dialed 911 to report a suicide attempt by Kyle Howard.

□ □ □

Sirens. . . . An ambulance. . . . Red lights flashing. . . . Two attendants and a stretcher. . . . White walls. . . . A linoleum-tiled floor.

A young intern grabbed for a plastic tube, pushed it up Kyle's nose, through his pharynx and throat, down the esophagus, into his stomach. Then, with a resident giving instructions, the intern squirted salt water up the tube and began sucking it out with a syringe.

"Blood pressure at one-forty over eighty," a voice reported. "Thirty respirations per minute. Pulse at one-ten."

As the doctors worked, Kyle drifted in and out of consciousness.

"Vital signs are good. Blood pressure down to one-thirty, pulse at ninety-five."

The intern kept sucking.

"Twenty respirations per minute."

"Get an IV ready for his arm."

"Blood pressure at one-twenty-five. Pulse at ninety."

Ten minutes after it had begun, the procedure was done.

"That's it," the resident said. "We'll save him."

Chapter 19

Monday morning. The day after the rain.
Richard Marritt stared at the thin colored
lines marking the map of Manhattan on his
office wall. Blue for Ethel Purcell. Green for
Linda Taylor. Brown for Alison Schoenfeld.
Yellow for Elizabeth Wald. Susan Marino's
last hours were traced in orange. Five women
dead. How many more?

Maybe I've gotten too close to the investigation, the detective pondered. Maybe I'm
missing the total picture by being too involved. Or maybe I'm not close enough. There
are a hundred detectives out in the field, and
instead of sitting behind a desk, maybe I
should be out there with them.

A young cop assigned to the case—one of
many whose name Marritt didn't know—came
into the office and handed the detective a
computer printout headed Cross-Index—Dr.
Doom. Every name entered in the computer
since it went on line had been classified by
category—former sex offenders, mental hospi-

211

tal releasees, and so on. Each name that appeared in more than one category was flagged immediately and brought to Marritt's attention. As he scanned the list, an entry at the bottom of the last page caught his eye:

Kyle Howard
Code 9–7/27
Code 4–7/21–P3

"Code 9" meant an attempted suicide on "7/27"—July 27, just one day earlier. "Code 4" indicated that, on July 21, someone had forwarded the individual's name to police investigators. The tip had been given a number three priority rating—"if-and-when"—by the officer taking the call.

Most of the double entries on the computer printout involved released mental hospital patients or suspects with a history of violent criminal conduct. Kyle Howard appeared to be a different matter. Curious, Marritt crossed the floor to a file cabinet at the far end of the room and leafed through the drawers until he came to the report he wanted:

July 21—Detective Louis Vairo

Name of suspect: Kyle Howard
Address: 212 West 88th Street
        New York, NY 10024
Telephone: 875-0174

Dear Hannah

Reported by: Hannah Wade
Address: 341 West 70th Street
New York, NY 10023
Telephone: 877-3124

Complainant telephoned to report that, after each of the murders under investigation, she received dead flowers sent anonymously through the mail. She believes these flowers were sent by Kyle Howard (a white male, approximate age 35), and that Mr. Howard has been obsessed with her for years. However, complainant acknowledges that Mr. Howard has made no threats and has not been violent toward her, and that to her knowledge he has broken no law. Also, when pressed, she conceded that the dates on which the flowers were received might not coincide fully with the murders. In my opinion, this lead does not require immediate attention and should be followed up only when time allows.

Except for the dead flowers, it really didn't amount to anything. And the flowers were speculative. Still, it was worth a look. Returning to his desk, the detective picked up the telephone and dialed downstairs for Jim Dema. "I'd like you to check up on someone named Kyle Howard," he instructed when the younger cop had come on the wire. "He tried to commit suicide yesterday. . . . That's right. Find out what hospital they took him to, and whether he's still there. If he is, I'll pay him a visit. . . . Not really, but I think it's time I got off my ass. And set up an appointment for me with a woman named Hannah Wade. She lives at Three-forty-one West Seventieth Street. . . . Early this afternoon—right after lunch, if possible."

□ □ □

The room was airy and well lit. There were four beds but two were empty, and the only other patient spent most of his time sleeping. As hospitals go, Kyle told himself, it wasn't bad. Except he didn't want to be there; he'd wanted it to be over.

And now, he wasn't sure.

Why couldn't Hannah simply be his friend? She was friends with other men. Why couldn't—

"Excuse me, Mr. Howard?"

Kyle looked up. One of the nurses and an unidentified man stood hovering over him.

"Mr. Howard, my name is Richard Marritt. I'm with the New York City Police Department. I'd like to ask you a few questions."

Lying back on the bed, Kyle closed his eyes. It was part of the indignity of attempting suicide. Everyone knew, and he had to talk with all of them—interns, psychiatrists, and now the police.

"I've spoken with Dr. Nimic," Kyle heard the cop saying, "and he's given me some background information. There are just a few things more I'd like to discuss with you."

The nurse left. Marritt reached for a metal-framed chair with a vinyl cushion and drew it close to the bed.

"Mr. Howard, the doctors tell me that you took an overdose of medication. Is that true?"

"Yes."

"What did you take?"

"Everything that was in my medicine cabinet."

"And what was that?"

"Aspirin, Comtrex, gentian violet—nothing very exciting."

"Why did you do it?"

"I was upset."

"Do you know how you got here?"

"I'm not sure. I got groggy and passed out. I guess someone called an ambulance."

"Do you know who?"

"I . . . I suppose it was someone named Hannah Wade."

"And who is Hannah Wade?"

There was no answer.

"Did you take the pills to go to sleep?"

"No."

"Did you take them to kill yourself?"

"I guess. . . . Sometimes I get tired of suffering and want to end it. I wasn't thinking clearly. I was upset."

"So you acted more on impulse than on a plan. Is that right?"

"I didn't really think about what I was doing. I just did it."

"And what are you planning to do now?"

Kyle's fingers began to lock and unlock together. "I guess I'd like it if everyone left me alone and let me go back to my apartment."

"What is it, exactly, that you like about Miss Wade?"

"I. . . . That's really not something I want to talk about."

"How do you know what sort of person she is?"

"I've known her. Ever since I was sixteen years old, I've known her."

"Have you known her well?"

"In some ways, yes. . . . Look, I appreciate what everyone at the hospital has done for me. I'm all right."

"I understand that, Mr. Howard. And I'm only trying to help. Did you ever send flowers of any kind to Hannah Wade?"

"No."

"Are you sure?"

A look of indignation flashed. "I sent her cards, and a book I wrote. I loved her. But I never sent flowers."

"Not even dead ones?"

"Why would anyone send dead flowers?"

Marritt weighed the response, then answered with another question. "Do you know what I think, Mr. Howard? From what the doctors and staff psychiatrist tell me, I don't think you ever believed you could win Miss Wade over. I think you simply decided to insert yourself into her life to torment her."

"That's ridiculous."

"Is it?"

"Why would I do that?"

"I don't know. Maybe you're mad at her for something she did, or didn't do, years ago. Maybe it's your way of asking for help. I'm not a psychiatrist. But my sense of the situation is that she's not available, and you'd be better off pursuing someone else."

"Can I go home now?"

"If you want. But if I could, I'd like to ask one favor. This afternoon I'm going to see Miss Wade. I'd like very much to be able to tell her that, from now on, you'll leave her alone."

There was a pause that seemed to last an eternity.

"What do you say, Mr. Howard?"

"All right."

"Thank you. And if it's any consolation, this woman might not be all that great. You don't know for sure what she's like at seven in the morning. And believe me, women are different at seven. I know; I'm married."

For the first time, Kyle half smiled.

"If you want to talk to someone," the detective concluded, "there's help available at the hospital. My instinct tells me you're decent enough. Take care of yourself."

□ □ □

Hannah sat in her apartment, with the television on, waiting. It was one P.M. She never watched daytime soaps, and didn't know why she was watching now except she was nervous. Detective Marritt should be there at any minute. That's what the cop who'd telephoned to set up the interview had told her. On the TV screen, a husband and wife were plotting to murder the wife's former husband. I should turn it off, Hannah decided. God forbid, a cop should walk in while I'm watching soap operas on televison.

The intercom sounded.

"Who is it?" she demanded, speaking into the mouthpiece.

"Richard Marritt, New York City Police Department."

Hannah buzzed him in, and waited for the sound of footsteps on the stairs. Then the doorbell rang, and she let him into her apartment.

"Good afternoon, Miss Wade. I'm Richard Marritt."

For a moment they stood still, facing each

other. I've read about him, Hannah told herself. That's funny; I've read about him in the newspapers.

Instant charm, Marritt realized, evaluating the woman in front of him. Now it was easier to understand Kyle Howard's obsession.

Hannah led him into the living room. The detective began when he was seated.

"Miss Wade, I've just visited Kyle Howard in the hospital. Physically, he's fine. Emotionally, the doctors say he's turned a corner. Most suicide attempts fall into the gesture category. Here, it appears as though Mr. Howard was trying to set up a situation where you showed your love by saving him. It worked to the extent he got your attention, but coming that close to death scared him. I think he'll leave you alone from now on."

"Are you sure?"

"Nothing's for sure, but the hospital plans to seek him out for continued treatment. The alternative would be for him to accept his depression, shrivel up and die, and I doubt that will happen. The suicide gesture was his cry for help."

Hannah sat silent, a mixture of skepticism and hope running through her. Kyle had done his penance. Maybe now he'd stay out of her life.

"There's one thing more," Marritt continued. "The written report on your call to the police mentioned something about dead flowers. Could you tell me about them?"

"What would you like to know?"

"Everything you remember."

"All right. Sometimes it seems a little silly, like I'm blowing everything out of proportion. But five times now, I've gotten a package in the mail. Each time, it's the stem and leaves of a long-stemmed rose wrapped in plain brown paper. The stems are headless, with lots of thorns. And each time, there's a card with letters I don't understand."

"Letters?"

"That's right. Wait, I'll show you." Marritt stayed on the sofa. Hannah stood up, crossed to the bedroom, and returned moments later with two cards. "Here. The one with the crease came with the second rose; I bent the corner by accident. The other came with rose number five."

"And the cards that are missing?"

"I threw them out."

"What about the roses?"

"I threw them out, too."

Holding card number five by the edges, Marritt stared at the letters: *THHIRWRDNK.*

"Do you have any idea what that means?"

"No," she answered.

"And all the cards were the same?"

"Yes. And they came in the mail, one after each murder."

"Are you positive?"

220

"I think so."

"Miss Wade, 'I think so' is different from being positive. Let me ask another question. Were any of the packages postmarked before the public announcement of the corresponding murder?"

"I don't remember."

Marritt took a breath and let it out slowly. "Okay. To be honest, I don't think there's any connection between the flowers and the murders. But right now we're desperate, so if it makes you feel better, we'll check the cards you still have for fingerprints."

"I feel kind of silly."

"Don't worry about it. The only thing is, you'll have to come back to the precinct house with me for a set of elimination prints. What that means is, I'll take your prints and send them to the lab along with the cards. Then the lab will discount your prints, and by the process of elimination, whatever is left belongs to the person who sent the roses."

"And after that?"

"If the sender's prints match Dr. Doom's, you'll be a media superstar and the most protected police witness in the history of New York. If not, you're on your own."

Back at the precinct house, Marritt brought Hannah upstairs to his office and gestured for her to take a seat. Then he exited the room, leaving her with her thoughts. It was strange, really. Reading the newspapers, she'd had the image of a well-oiled police machine pursuing Dr. Doom. Yet here she was, in a dingy room on the second floor of a plain brick building off Columbus Avenue. If this was the height of police technology—

Marritt returned, interrupting her thoughts. Opening a narrow metal case, he drew out a black ink pad and a three-by-eight-inch cardboard card marked by two rows of boxes, five boxes in each row.

"This will only take a minute," he said. Wordlessly, he reached for Hannah's hand, took her right thumb, and rolled it along the ink pad before pressing it against the upper-lefthand-corner box marked R. THUMB. Then he repeated the process . . . right index finger . . . right middle . . . right ring . . . right little. . . . Hannah's left hand followed. "There's a ladies' room on the ground floor," he said when they'd finished. "Soap and water will get the ink off your fingers."

"Is there anything else?"

"Not at the moment. But believe me, we'll be in touch if the results are positive."

Hannah left. Marritt picked up the telephone, buzzed for a patrolman, and instructed him to take the cards plus Hannah's prints to the police laboratory on 20th Street. Then he telephoned ahead to speak with Danny Keegan, the lab technician who'd been handling Dr. Doom since the third murder. Keegan was the best fingerprint expert on the force. A heavyset, balding man who'd been a rookie with Marritt twenty years earlier, he knew his stuff. "Don't worry about a thing," he advised when apprised of the fingerprint cards coming his way. "I'll check 'em out."

"I'm worried about lots of things," Marritt retorted. "How soon can I have results?"

"Card number five—the one that came after the last murder—won't be a problem. Susan Marino was killed last week, so iodine fuming will get us prints in less than an hour. Card number two is a little more complicated. You're talking about June, five or six weeks ago. The amino acids have dried up and sunk into the paper fibers."

"Which means what?"

"For card number two, I'll need forty-eight hours. Ninhydrin is the only thing I know that'll work."

When the conversation was over, Marritt summoned Dema for an update on the day's events. Nothing new had developed on the younger cop's end. Then the detective recounted his visits with Hannah Wade and Kyle Howard.

"Why didn't you take Kyle Howard's fingerprints?" Dema queried.

"I thought about it, but he didn't seem like a killer. Besides, I didn't bring a fingerprint kit to the hospital with me."

Danny Keegan called back at four o'clock.

"Richard; T-H-H-I-R-W-R-D-N-K. What's that all about?"

"If I knew, I'd tell you," Marritt said wearily. "I think it's nothing but a guy who has a crush on a girl and sends her dead roses."

"Well, tell the girl that whoever sent the roses wiped his prints off the card first. The only thing I got off card number five was Hannah Wade's prints."

"Are you sure?"

"Positive. I'll let you know about card number two on Wednesday."

The rest of the afternoon passed without incident. "It's quitting time," the detective told Dema at five-thirty. "I think I'll saddle my horse and ride off into the sunset."

As usual, the subway was jammed. Marritt spent the first half hour of the ride reading his newspaper. Then he switched to people-watching, taking note of a woman who was wearing jogging shoes with her business suit. She probably slipped into a more formal pair at the office. He wondered why the bulk of women's shoes weren't more comfortable. The train rumbled on . . . Woodhaven Boulevard . . . Continental Avenue. . . . At 169th Street, the detective made a mental note of the train's proximity to Memorial Hospital. Part of his training as a cop, and family man, was to know which hospitals were nearby and which had the best emergency rooms. Just after six-thirty, he arrived home.

"David, be quiet and listen to me," his wife was saying.

"I can talk and listen at the same time."

"Well, you're not listening hard enough, because your room's a mess."

Following the voices into the kitchen, Marritt kissed his wife and David. "Where's Jonathan?"

"Upstairs, cleaning his room, like David should be."

"That's not my job," David objected.

"What's your job?" Marritt queried.

"Going to school and going to camp."

"Well, now you've got a new job—cleaning your room."

"And if I don't?"

"Then you go to bed hungry, without any pizza."

There was silence, followed by a touch of respect in David's voice. "How did you know we're having pizza for dinner?"

Marritt gestured toward a two-foot-square cardboard box on the kitchen table. "I'm a detective. I can tell by the shape of the box."

Chapter 20

THE DAY AFTER THE POLICE TOOK HER FINGER-
prints, Hannah spent the morning thinking
about Kyle. Not that she thought he was "Dr.
Doom"; she didn't. But trying to push him out
of her psyche was like heeding the injunction,
"Don't think about a purple elephant." So
instructed, it was impossible to push the
elephant out of mind.

Marritt telephoned during the afternoon to
report that "card number five" had no fingerprints but her own. Late in the day, Hannah
taught two dance classes, and that night,
went out for dinner with Fergy. They'd spent
a lot of time together lately. He was one of
the few people she felt comfortable with;
maybe the only one.

Mexican food; Columbus Avenue in the
Seventies. Dipping taco chips into salsa picante,
Hannah recounted her trip to the precinct
house the previous afternoon. "Whoever sent
the roses didn't leave fingerprints," she
reported.

Fergy ordered a second margarita—he'd downed his first pretty quickly—and Hannah continued with a description of Marritt's office, particularly the map of Manhattan on the detective's wall.

"You know something, Banana? You're sexy when I've had a drink."

"I'm sexy all the time."

"I know. I guess I just have to have a drink before I can tell you."

They gave each other funny looks. Fergy made comments like that all the time; he'd done it for years. But at the moment, he seemed more vulnerable than usual.

"You're wonderful," he added. "Wonderful is a good word, one of the better words in the English language." And then he drew back, as though fearful of crossing the line by which Hannah delineated the relationships in her life. "Anyway, Banana, did I tell you that I ran into Arthur Montgomery last week?"

"Who's Arthur Montgomery?"

"A truly legendary bastard. For years, the chief executive officer at Peterson Brownfield— that's where I used to work—was a man named Chester Ross. Twenty years ago, when Ross was at the peak of his power, he took Montgomery under his wing, brought him along, and treated him like a son. Every Friday afternoon they'd play chess together in Ross's office. Keep in mind, Chester Ross was one of the most important men on Wall

Street, but once a week he cleared his calendar to play chess with Montgomery. The years went by. Montgomery rose in the firm hierarchy, and Ross got old. The week Montgomery was named chief executive officer, he told Ross he was too busy to play chess with him anymore."

"Sounds like a real sweetheart."

"You got it. Anyway, I ran into Montgomery on Park Avenue, and he had no idea who I was except that I was a former peon at Peterson Brownfield. Just for the heck of it, I lied and told him I was currently employed by the Enforcement Division of the Securities and Exchange Commission. After that, you should have seen how friendly he was. He put his arm around me and everything. I can't tell you how satisfying it was to see him grovel."

The waiter came and took their meal orders. Having started with Arthur Montgomery, Fergy continued his description of upper management at Peterson Brownfield & Company:

Lawrence Winstable—"A pompous ass. When Winstable and his wife moved to Scarsdale, they needed newspaper to pack their breakables. Instead of collecting it like normal people, they sent the butler out to buy two dozen copies of the Sunday *Times*."

David Parker—"One of the meanest, worst-dressed men who ever lived. When it comes to neckties, he has an eye for color like Stevie

Wonder. Parker's secretary voted for Jesse Jackson in the 1984 Democratic Primary, so he fired her."

Franklin Winter—"The quintessential WASP; social register; on the board of directors of every major museum in New York. Actually, Winter has a fairly good sense of humor, but he's an idiot. If it weren't for his sense of humor, he'd have no sense at all."

Microwave ovens being what they were, dinner arrived shortly. Fergy declined a third margarita ("I've never been able to drink enough to have a hangover"), and turned the conversation back to Hannah's session with Richard Marritt. Then, inevitably, they drifted to Kyle.

"I think he's gone now," she said. "At least, I hope so."

"And the roses?"

"Probably he sent them each time he read about a murder in the newspaper. I don't know; maybe they're not connected to the murders at all."

After dinner they went for a walk. Three new stores had opened on Columbus Avenue— one that specialized in champagne truffles, a boutique called The Kept Woman, and a health food shop purporting to sell mother's milk.

"There's a full moon tonight," Fergy announced, gazing skyward.

"Fergy, that's a streetlight."

"Sorry. I guess I had one margarita too many."

They walked for an hour, talking, watching other people, watching people watch them. At one point, Hannah took Fergy's arm as they walked. She enjoyed being with him, not just tonight, always. She was never lonely when they were together. Almost without noticing, she dropped her arm so they were touching hands. What was it Fergy had told her that night they'd had dinner at Metropolis? "You're always X-ing everyone, Banana." Something like that. She'd ponder that one, think it over.

Around ten-thirty, he brought her home. "Let me ask you something," he said when they reached her building. "Does tonight mean it's all right for us to hold hands?"

It was a funny way for him to put the question. But then, she couldn't recall their having held hands before.

"I guess so."

"Fantastic!"

And then she kissed him. They'd kissed good night lots of times, pro forma kisses between friends. This one was different. She really kissed him. She drew close, put her arms around him, put her lips to his, and kept them there for a long time.

"Banana, that was wonderful."

"Our first kiss," she told him.

□ □ □

It was over. He'd tried, done everything he could. Now, whatever else happened, Hannah was gone. Oblivious to the passersby who swirled along Columbus Avenue, Kyle trod slowly with his head down. That's all; it's done. And no one really could understand. Even the people who wrote songs about love—Irving Berlin, Cole Porter, Jerome Kern, all of them—what did they know? They should rewrite their lyrics to include headaches, nausea, all the symptoms of love.

Anyway, at least he was out of the hospital. Be thankful for little things. How did you feel when you saw Hannah with other men? That was a question the hospital psychiatrist had asked. How do you think I felt, asshole. That's what I should have told him.

"Once, I saw a woman on the street, kissing this guy. It was a long open-mouthed kiss. And until I got closer, I thought it was Hannah."

"And?" the psychiatrist had wanted to know.

"I'm glad it wasn't. Kissing in public is wrong."

"How did you feel when Hannah got married?"

"Terrible."

"Did you know about it beforehand?"

"Yes."

"Did you go to the wedding?"

"Of course not. I wasn't invited."

He doesn't know me; he doesn't know

Hannah. How can he help when he doesn't understand. Besides, there's nothing he could do. Hannah is gone. I just have to treat it as though she died; a piece of my soul gone forever.

It was getting late, and Kyle hadn't brought a jacket with him. Even in July, the night air could be cool.

When Hannah got her divorce, God, I was happy. I guess it was like being reborn. Maybe now if I could undergo some sort of transformation, realize a new dimension. I wish I were Fergy. Then, at least— Forget it. Hannah's gone.

It was growing cooler.

I really don't want to go home alone. I wish there was someone I could be with or call. I wonder if Hannah will ever forgive me for what I've done. She should; happy people are more forgiving than others. My life—how would I describe it? The seeds that were sown—that's a good start. The seeds that were sown early in my life started to grow, but they were ugly weeds, not flowers. Stop it. Don't think like that. It's not the end of the world. That's what the psychiatrist said. Nothing is the end of the world except the end of the world. Life goes on.

□ □ □

Two A.M.
Dora Chapman stood by the stoop of her

apartment building and marveled at the fact that her evening hadn't turned out badly after all. Most of the men she met in bars after midnight were, let's be honest, the kind of men you met in bars after midnight. But Arnold was different—brighter than average and very nice.

"I know this sounds silly," she told him after he'd walked her home. "I'd invite you up for a drink, but I can't because of Dr. Doom."

"I understand. Maybe we could get together another time."

"I'd love to. Let me give you my number." Dora fumbled through her purse. "Do you have a pen?"

"I'm afraid not."

"And I'm not listed in the phone book. What the hell, I have a pen upstairs."

She led the way; Arnold followed. "I hate to be rude. It's just, with all the coverage these murders have had in the newspapers, it's good to be careful."

"I understand."

At the door to her apartment, Dora considered asking him to wait in the corridor while she went inside and wrote her number down. But at that point it would have been too embarrassing.

"Now that you're here, you might as well have some coffee," she said as they stepped inside.

234

"Actually, I'm not much of a coffee drinker.
Water is fine."

"How about ice cream?"

"It's a thought. What kind?"

"Vanilla, and I think there's some chocolate chip in the back of the freezer."

"On second thought, I'll pass. Just water,
with ice."

Dora took a glass from the cupboard, filled
it with water and ice, and handed it to him.
Then she took the vanilla ice cream, put two
scoops in a dish, and congratulated herself on
the fact that under the Dora Chapman Organ-
izational System she never ran out of Häagen-
Dazs. Everything was fine—except then she
noticed that the kitchen faucet was still running, and she was sure she'd turned it off
after filling Arnold's glass.

So she turned it off again.

"You have a very funny body," he told her.
"Do you know that?"

"Pardon?"

"I wasn't going to mention it, but you're
shaped like a pear."

Stay calm, Dora told herself.

Arnold reached over and turned the water
on again. "You don't mind, do you?"

"No."

"Of course you don't. I didn't think you
would. After all, you've used all your intellec-
tual powers to ascertain that running water
isn't a major problem. Isn't that right?"

235

"Yes, that's right."

"And you've decided that, whatever I do, you'll go along with it as long as I promise not to hurt you."

"Yes."

"Did I ever tell you about the time I lost my virginity."

"No."

"I didn't think so. And I didn't tell you about going through my mother's bureau and finding nude photos of her and her boyfriend either, did I?"

"No, you didn't."

"You're a dead woman, Dora."

"Please don't hurt me."

"You're not listening, Dora. I said you're dead."

Chapter 21

THE SUBWAY COMING INTO MANHATTAN WAS jammed. Midway between Queens Plaza and Ely Avenue, the air conditioning broke down. Then the lights went dim. By the time Marritt reached the precinct house, his shirt and jacket were drenched with sweat. "And it's Wednesday," he told Dema. "My day off." Together, they reviewed the latest computer printouts and investigative reports. Then Marritt reached for his copy of the *Daily News*.

"Listen to this! I read it on the subway coming in: 'Sources close to the investigation say senior officials are questioning whether computer technology and other modern forensic devices have been properly used in pursuing Dr. Doom. It might not be [Lieutenant Richard] Marritt's fault, said one investigator, but a lot of questions are being asked.' "

Gritting his teeth, Marritt tossed the newspaper aside. "I really don't need this garbage."

"It's not that bad," Dema offered. "The article says it's not your fault."

"Might not be my fault," the detective corrected. "I know what they're saying. Even a dog knows the difference between being tripped over and getting kicked."

Several telephone calls and a conference with the borough commander took up the rest of the morning. At noon Marritt declined an invitation to have lunch with the precinct captain, and sent out for sandwiches instead. "I didn't have lunch with him because I didn't want to have lunch with him," he explained to Dema over a pastrami sandwich. "Lunch is very important to me; I didn't want to ruin it."

The afternoon went on. More paper work. Dema went out to buy a scrapbook for the ever-burgeoning pile of Dr. Doom newspaper clippings. Marritt made another series of telephone calls and reviewed a stack of investigative reports. At two o'clock, over coffee, they caucused again.

"You know something?" the detective told his partner. "Sometimes I wonder how I'd react if I actually met Dr. Doom. Here's a guy, a murderer, a real monster. I've faced killers before, but never anyone like him . . ." His voice trailed off, then picked up again. "What it comes down to is, five women are dead. All we need is number six, and the entire city will go crazy."

The telephone rang.

"Twentieth precinct," Marritt said, picking up the receiver.

"Richard? This is Keegan, down at the fingerprint lab."

"What's up?"

"Card number two—the one you got from Hannah Wade. The fingerprints match."

"What do you mean, the fingerprints match?"

"It's him. The fingerprints on the card belong to Dr. Doom."

□ □ □

Contrary to her general penchant for neatness, Hannah had a thing about vacuuming the apartment. Washing dishes was fine; making the bed and doing laundry were palatable. But it was only reluctantly, and no more than once a month, that Hannah picked up a vacuum cleaner. Today was the day, and as she worked, her mind wandered.

In about an hour she had to be at the studio for a class of five-year-olds. Children that age didn't really dance; they bounced to music. Then, after the five-year-olds—

The telephone sounded.

Another ring.

Hannah wasn't sure how many rings that totaled; she might have missed a few because of the vacuum cleaner. Running to the bedroom, she picked up the receiver.

"Miss Wade, this is Richard Marritt of the New York City Police Department."

"Yes?"

"There were two fingerprints on the card you gave us. Both match."

Hannah struggled to catch her breath.

"Miss Wade? Are you there?"

"Yes."

"What I'm saying is, after we eliminated your prints, two latent fingerprints were still there. Both of them match up with Dr. Doom."

Hannah's hands began to shake.

"We're looking for Kyle Howard," she heard Marritt saying. "He's not in his apartment. Do you have any idea where he is?"

"I think. . . . He works at a bookstore. It's called Omnibus."

"How do you spell that?"

"O-m-n-i-b-u-s. It's at Broadway and Tenth Street, or something like that."

There was a pause while the detective wrote down the name and address.

"Miss Wade, I'm going to Omnibus. Don't leave your apartment until you hear from me again. And don't let Kyle Howard into your apartment."

Then the line went dead, and Hannah was alone. And there was something wrong with her—she knew that—because the first thing she thought of was "I have to leave the apartment; I've got a class to teach in less than an hour." Cancel the class, stupid. Hannah picked up the receiver, dialed the studio, and left word that classes were off. Then she went to the kitchen and, when she got there, realized she didn't know why she was there or what she wanted, except she was standing with the refrigerator door open. Calm down, she told herself. Don't lose control. What to do? And then she realized she should do what she always did when she was in trouble and needed help. She picked up the telephone and called Fergy.

He was at work. But when Hannah told him what was happening and that she was scared, he promised to drop everything and come right over.

□   □   □

Marritt and Dema sat in the back seat of the blue and white patrol car as it streaked down Eleventh Avenue. The siren wailed; red lights were flashing.

"Let's go over it again," the detective instructed. "All I want from this guy is fingerprints."

"Without a warrant?"

"Don't worry. I'll handle that."

"I don't understand. Why not just arrest him?"

"Because if he's the wrong guy, the press will go bonkers."

At Eleventh Avenue and 14th Street, the driver turned east.

"Cut the siren," Marritt ordered. "The less attention, the better."

Eighth Avenue . . . Avenue of the Americas . . . Fifth Avenue . . . University Place. . . . At the corner of Broadway and Tenth Street, the patrol car came to a halt. Marritt got out and half walked, half ran into the bookstore. Dema followed. Inside, seemingly endless rows of books were stacked on floor-to-ceiling shelves. Signs labeled History, Literature, Religion, Music, Political Science, and so on demarcated the store.

Marritt looked around. Dressed in a plaid shirt and slacks, Kyle Howard stood behind a cash register near the door. "That's him," the detective told Dema. "Stay here. Don't let him out of your sight."

Three large tables piled high with books dominated the front of the store. Moving toward them, Marritt surveyed what was there. No good. Maybe. No. No.

A book titled *The Cathedral Phantom* caught his eye. The dust jacket was white, clean, and very glossy. Picking it up, the detective took a deep breath, exhaled, and walked to an isolated area at the rear of the store. There, he reached into his pocket for a handkerchief and wiped the dust jacket clean. Then, holding the book at the edges, he returned to the checkout counter. There were two lines and two cash registers. Aware that his heart was beating rapidly, he stepped to the end of Kyle's line and stared. The man behind the register didn't look like a mass murderer, but five women hadn't thought so either.

The line moved slowly. Finally, the detective's turn came.

Kyle looked up. Eye contact. Marritt handed him the book.

"That's ten dollars and seventy-seven cents."

Wordlessly, the detective reached for his wallet and drew out eleven dollars. Kyle took the money, rang the sale up on the cash register, and handed Marritt his change. Then, without visible emotion, he reached for a plastic bag, shoved the book inside, and handed it back to the detective.

Cradling his prize, Marritt moved away from the register to the spot where Dema was waiting. "Stay here. I'm going to the fingerprinting lab. Don't let Kyle Howard out of this store."

"What do I do if he tries to leave?"

"Pick him up for questioning; you choose the charge."

"Hey, Richard, that was nice work, getting his fingerprints on the book just now."

"Yeah. It's a good thing I'm on the side of the law."

Marritt left.

Dema stood by the south wall. A young woman with long brown hair tied up in a bun came out of the stockroom and approached the cash registers. "Coffee break," she told Kyle.

Giving her his place, Kyle stepped off the platform, glanced toward Dema, and disappeared into the stockroom behind closed doors.

Chapter 22

"HELLO, BANANA."

Hannah stood in the doorway to her apartment, looking at Fergy, and smiled. "I'm glad you're here."

"Me too. It sounds as though you need a friend."

"More than a friend. I'm confused. I'm scared." And then she realized they were still standing in the doorway. "Come on in."

The late-afternoon sun radiated streaks of light across the living room floor. They sat on the sofa.

"I don't know," Hannah heard herself saying. "I just don't know. Kyle, Dr. Doom, long ago, now. These past few weeks, everything has been cascading down. I've found myself thinking about things that happened years ago, wishing I'd lived my life differently, telling myself I should have started working out my problems long ago. And then I tell myself I can't do anything about the past. I can't change what happened yesterday, let alone ten years ago, and I say to myself, working things out now would be better than never doing it at all."

"And where do I fit in?"

"Anywhere you want. Fergy, neither of us is that young anymore. If we get involved— How did I get into this mess? I'm not making sense, am I?"

"I don't know. Keep talking."

"What I'm trying to say is, if you and I get involved, we're both going to put a lot of pressure on ourselves to make this relationship be the one. And even if you love me, maybe I don't love myself. But if we both try . . ."

And then Hannah realized that talking was stupid, because she was looking at Fergy and she was crazy about him as a friend and maybe they could handle it as lovers after all. And if that worked, who knows. She gave Fergy a kind of funny look, and put her arms around him. They'd kissed before but never like this; not even their first kiss the night before. And Hannah figured it just might be that something good would come out of the whole nightmare she'd been living.

"Fergy, let's make love."

Taking his hand, she led him to the bedroom. It was smaller than he'd remembered it, nicely decorated. It made him think of lace and flowers. The window was open, with the hint of a breeze floating in. Fergy's hands began to tremble.

"Are you all right?"

"I'm fine, Banana. This is spectacular."

Reaching up, Hannah undid the buttons on Fergy's shirt. He arched his shoulders, and it fell to the floor.

"You're next."

Hannah lifted the sweater over her head, revealing her breasts as they swelled in her bra. They moved near the bed and continued to disrobe, until finally they stood naked, fully exposed. Fergy reached out and touched her cheek. He was larger than Hannah had realized; a little heavier, more muscular, too. He was looking at her in a way that made her nervous; she didn't know why.

"Should we take the phone off the hook?"

"All right," she answered.

"Hannah, I think I'm in love with you."

"It's very strange."

"Strange, but wonderful. The heart has its reasons which reason does not know."

Hannah smiled. She smiled because the phrase Fergy had just used sounded nice, and because she remembered he'd said it to her once before—in the park, after Kyle had run away from them three days ago. Wherever Kyle was, if he managed to find out that she and Fergy were in bed together—

The heart has its reasons. . . . Hannah began to play the words through her mind.

247

Kyle had sent the roses; she knew that. The fingerprints were Kyle's; they had to be. The heart has its reasons. . . . Hannah tried to spell it out, but it was hard because her thoughts were spinning. . . . The heart—TH. The heart has its reasons—THHIR. What was the rest of it? Kyle's fingerprints were on the card. . . . No. Marritt had said Dr. Doom's prints were on the card. And Fergy's prints had been on the card, the one from June, because she'd shown it to him that night in her apartment when they'd looked at her high school yearbook together. So Fergy's prints were on the card, and what was it that Marritt had told her on the telephone? "There were two fingerprints on the card you gave us. Both match." Not one matches and one doesn't. Both of them match up with Dr. Doom. So it was Dr. Doom who had written THHIRWRDNK, which was a perfect acronym for what Fergy had just told her for the second time in three days—"The heart has its reasons which reason does not know."

Hannah gasped.

Something she was very afraid of was showing in Fergy's eyes.

□ □ □

Flashing his badge, Richard Marritt moved past the cop on duty at the entrance to the Police Academy. Through the lobby. The wait for an elevator seemed endless. Finally, a bell sounded, and heavy stainless steel doors opened. Second floor. . . . Third. . . . On the eighth floor, the detective exited and turned right, down a wide corridor. At the door to the fingerprint lab, Danny Keegan was waiting.

"Danny, I've got a book I want you to check for prints, and do it in a hurry."

Reaching for the bag that Marritt offered, Keegan peered inside. "Okay. Give me ten minutes, and the prints are yours."

They walked quickly down another corridor to a ten-by-twenty-foot room with scuffed linoleum and dingy gray walls. A long metal table ran adjacent to the door. File cabinets fronted the opposite wall. Keegan took a bottle of Krazy Glue off the table and held it aloft. "Here we are—state-of-the-art technology."

"Danny, this is serious. Don't fuck around."

Gesturing toward a cylindrical glass container at the end of the table, the technician went on. "That's a desiccator. Look inside and you'll see cotton pads soaked in sodium hydroxide." Lifting the desiccator lid, he squirted a teaspoon's worth of Krazy Glue onto the pads. White smoke began to rise. "The active ingredient in all these superglues is cyanoacrylate. Sodium hydroxide turns it into a fume state, and the fumes attach to the oxygen molecules a person's fingers leave behind."

Marritt's eyes began to burn. Keegan

reached for the book, removed the dust jacket, and dropped it into the desiccator, then put the lid back on. "Stand back. These fumes can be hard on the mucous membranes and eyes."

Five minutes passed. Marritt shifted nervously from one foot to the other. "It's him, Danny. I'm sure. The guy who handed me this book is Dr. Doom."

Four minutes to go . . . three minutes . . . two minutes and thirty seconds. . . . Finally, Keegan lifted the lid and reached inside. "Okay, Richard. What we have here are plastic outlines of this guy's prints. All we got to do now is sprinkle on powder, and the prints are yours."

The detective waited. Keegan took a brush, dipped it into a jar of black powder, and ran it across the glossy white dust jacket. A series of fingerprints began to form.

"Judging by what I see here, we got at least a dozen near-perfect prints," the technician said confidently. "Both thumbs, a pinkie, eight or nine different fingers in all. Gimme the tape."

Marritt reached for a roll of clear plastic tape as instructed. Keegan unwound a strip, lay it across a print on the upper right-hand corner of the dust jacket, and pressed firmly down. Then he lifted the tape and pressed down again, this time on a heavy white card. Carefully, he repeated the process eleven times.

Twelve prints; twelve cards in all. "Nine different fingers," he told the detective. "You're missing a pinkie. Let's compare them with Dr. Doom."

Marritt's heart began to pound. Keegan reached for the fingerprints that had been found in the apartments of five murdered women.

"It's not him."

"What do you mean?"

"Richard, look for yourself. It's not him. The tented arches on the killer's thumbs are different from what you just gave me. So's the slant loop on his right ring finger. The prints don't match—none of them."

"But it's got to be him."

"Richard, I'm telling you. The guy you saw this afternoon left prints all over this book. Unless he's got twenty fingers, he's not Dr. Doom."

Another cop came into the room. "Lieutenant Marritt?"

"What is it?" the detective muttered.

"Sir, you're wanted on the telephone. There's been another murder."

Marritt struggled to maintain his composure.

"On West Fortieth Street, a woman named Dora Chapman. They found the body an hour ago."

Pull yourself together, the detective told himself. Don't let go.

"Sir, the police commissioner wants to talk with you immediately."

"Tell him I'm not available. I'm going to talk to someone about a dead rose."

□ □ □

Hannah sat on the edge of her bed, naked, with Fergy between her and the door.

"You sent the roses."

"What?"

"You sent the roses. The heart has its reasons which reason does not know."

"Hannah, that's silly."

"No, it isn't."

"Anyone could say that. It's from a seventeenth-century philosopher, Blaise Pascal."

"Pascal's been dead for three hundred years. He didn't send the roses." Don't show fear, Hannah told herself. Meet him head-on. "I'm onto you, Fergy. I know who you are."

"To what do you attribute this bizarre behavior?"

"It's not bizarre."

"Then let me rephrase the question and make it a statement. You're saying things that have very unhealthy implications."

"Really? Tell me about women, Fergy."

"I don't understand."

"Tell me about women. What do you think of them?"

"I don't know . . . I like women."

"If you were going to kill someone, who would you kill—a man or a woman?"

"You're being silly."

"I guess it would be easier for you to kill a woman. We're more defenseless than men. But I'm not worried, because I'm naked and Dr. Doom only kills women with their clothes on. Look at me, Fergy. Look at my body."

She was gathering strength, speaking in low level tones.

"Look at me, Fergy. What are you looking down for? Look at my body."

"Hannah, I don't like what you're doing."

"I'm sorry, Fergy, but you know how people are. They do the most unexpected things. When you open the doors to someone's mind, there's no telling what you'll find."

"Stop it."

"I can't stop. It's a compulsion; that's the sort of thing you'd understand."

He was weakening.

"And it's funny, Fergy. Everything I've heard about people like you is true. There's no way to know who you are."

Outside the bedroom, the apartment intercom sounded.

"Stay here, Fergy. I'll be back in a moment."

Fergy clung to the edge of the bed, his eyes transfixed, looking down. Hannah stood up and walked to the door. She could run into the corridor now, naked, but why bother. Fergy wasn't a threat; not anymore.

"Yes?" she said, pushing the intercom button.

"Miss Wade, this is Richard Marritt. I'd like to talk with you."

Hannah hit the buzzer.

"Don't worry, Fergy. I'll be back in a moment."

Ten seconds . . . twenty. . . .

Marritt's footsteps echoed on the stairs below.